PENGUIN 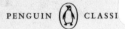 CLASSI

THE COMPLETE FABLES

AESOP probably lived in the middle part of the sixth century BC. A statement in Herodotus gives ground for thinking that he was a slave belonging to a citizen of Samos called Iadmon. Legend says that he was ugly and misshapen. There are many references to Aesop found in the Athenian writers: Aristophanes, Xenophon, Plato, Aristotle and others. It is not known whether he wrote down his fables himself, nor indeed how many of them are correctly attributed to his invention.

OLIVIA TEMPLE was born in London and educated at a convent grammar school in Hertfordshire. She has published extracts from her diary and written articles and reviews for a variety of magazines. She is a figurative painter, with works in private collections in Europe, America, Hong Kong and New Zealand.

ROBERT TEMPLE has a degree in Sanskrit and is the author of eight books, including a history of Chinese science. He translated the Babylonian *Epic of Gilgamesh*, which was produced at the Royal National Theatre in London in 1993, and has published several articles about the scientific works of Aristotle. His book *Conversations with Eternity* includes studies of ancient Greek oracles and divination techniques. He is also a television drama producer.

THE
PAUL HAMLYN
LIBRARY

DONATED BY

Lydia Barker

TO THE

BRITISH MUSEUM

opened December 2000

WITHDRAWN

The Complete Fables

AESOP

Translated by OLIVIA *and* ROBERT TEMPLE
With an Introduction by ROBERT TEMPLE

PENGUIN BOOKS

PENGUIN BOOKS

Published by the Penguin Group
Penguin Books Ltd, 27 Wrights Lane, London w8 5tz, England
Penguin Books USA Inc., 375 Hudson Street, New York, New York 10014, USA
Penguin Books Australia Ltd, Ringwood, Victoria, Australia
Penguin Books Canada Ltd, 10 Alcorn Avenue, Toronto, Ontario, Canada m4v 3b2
Penguin Books (NZ) Ltd, 182–190 Wairau Road, Auckland 10, New Zealand

Penguin Books Ltd, Registered Offices: Harmondsworth, Middlesex, England

This translation first published in Penguin Classics 1998
3 5 7 9 10 8 6 4 2

Copyright © Translation and Annotation, 1998 Robert and Olivia Temple
Copyright © Introduction, 1998 Robert Temple
All rights reserved

The moral right of the translators has been asserted

Set in 10/12.5pt Postscript Monotype Bembo
Typeset by Rowland Phototypesetting Ltd, Bury St Edmunds, Suffolk
Printed in England by Clays Ltd, St Ives plc

Except in the United States of America, this book is sold subject
to the condition that it shall not, by way of trade or otherwise, be lent,
re-sold, hired out, or otherwise circulated without the publisher's
prior consent in any form of binding or cover other than that in
which it is published and without a similar condition including this
condition being imposed on the subsequent purchaser

THE BRITISH MUSEUM
WITHDRAWN
THE PAUL HAMLYN LIBRARY

398. 2452 AES

For our godchildren
Camilla, Edward, Antony,
Niralie, Alice, Laurie,
Joshua and Benjamin
and also for Emma

Contents

Introduction

Aesop's Fables – what a ring it has to it! Of all the names of authors from Greek antiquity, Aesop is probably the best known, more so even than Homer. But it is ironical that Aesop's reputation should be so high when so little is accurately known about him or his work and when no complete translation of his fables has ever existed in English. He is rather like a movie star – everyone thinks they know him but in fact they only know him from certain roles he has played. The roles Aesop has played have been as a children's storyteller and as a clothes-horse for Victorian morals such as 'haste makes waste' and 'pride comes before a fall' – no such morals actually occur in Aesop at all. The animal stories which parents still buy in quantities for their children's birthdays bear little resemblance to the real Aesop fables. I hesitate to say 'the real Aesop', because so little is known about the historical Aesop that some have maintained that he never actually existed.

It seems, however, that he did exist. Although the ancient *Life of Aesop*, which existed before the time of Plato, consists largely of fantasy episodes of an already legendary figure, serious scholars like Aristotle and his school made attempts to sort out the fact from fiction and came up with the conclusion that Aesop was not a Phrygian (from Asia Minor), as commonly believed in their day, but was actually a native of the town of Mesembria, in Thrace on the Greek mainland, and that he lived for some time on the Island of Samos. (This information survives in fragments of Aristotle's lost *Constitution of Samos*.)

Aesop seems to have been a slave as a result of captivity. In Greek there were two different words for slaves, denoting whether a person had been born a slave (*doulos*) or had been captured in war and sold into slavery (*andrapodon*). Aesop was apparently in the latter category. But, despite this status, which rendered him liable to sale and deprived of all rights, Aesop appears to have lived the life largely of a personal clerk/secretary and even what we could call a confidential agent for his owners. He seems to have been a great wit, whose reputation for telling little animal tales in discussion and negotiation and scoring devastatingly clever points with them astonished and impressed his contemporaries. He thus became a legendary name around which all such witty animal tales clustered in later centuries, most of the surviving ones probably not actually written by him.

Aesop lived in the early sixth century BC, and one suggestion of his date of death is 564 BC, which may well be correct. One of the most famous courtesans of Greek antiquity was a woman named Doricha, better known by her nickname of Rhodopis, a Thracian who seems to have been seized in war at the same time as Aesop, since they became fellow-slaves. She (and possibly Aesop as well) was taken to Egypt, where she achieved fame all over the Mediterranean world for her irresistible beauty and charm. Charaxus of Mytilene in Lesbos, brother of the poetess Sappho, became infatuated with Rhodopis and bought her freedom at an enormous price. Charaxus was, at the time, engaged in a trading trip to Egypt, selling Lesbian wine. Sappho was furious with her brother because of this wild financial extravagance, and she wrote a poem ridiculing him. These historical facts help to anchor the dates of Aesop in some kind of chronological reality. The legends of Aesop's association with King Croesus, on the other hand, appear to be pure fiction, as does a false story that Aesop went to Delphi and was thrown from a cliff while he was telling the fable of 'The Eagle and the Scarab Beetle', Fable 4 in this volume. (So widespread was the popular belief in this last episode that it is referred to by Aristophanes in *The Wasps* (1446) so briefly in passing that he clearly knows that his audience will be familiar with all the details of the story; that was in 422 BC.)

Since the best of the Aesop fables are full of wit and jest, it is not surprising that they were great favourites of the comic playwright Aristophanes. He refers to Aesop and some of his fables many times in his surviving plays. Some references are intriguing in the clues they give us as to the state of the Aesopic material in his time. In *The Birds* (470), written in 414 BC, one of his characters complains to another that he has not heard of the ancient lineage of the birds 'because you've a blind uninquisitive mind, unaccustomed to poring over Aesop'. Thus we are led to presume that early collections of Aesop fables existed in book form. And two references in *The Wasps* are interesting: at 565 Aristophanes gives some indication of how the Aesop material was conceived, when he says: 'Some tell us a legend of days gone by, or a joke from Aesop, witty and sage . . .' And at 1255, two characters are speaking of drinking parties, one of them complaining about the violent behaviour and hangovers which they normally entail, but the other claims: 'Not if you drink with gentlemen, you know. They'll . . . tell some merry tale, a jest from Sybaris, or one of Aesop's, learned at the feast. And so the matter turns into a joke . . .' The other character replies: 'Oh, I'll learn plenty of those tales . . .'

These references show that the more refined drinking parties, or symposia, at Athens in the fifth century BC featured repartee and witty stories, and that people attending them who wanted to make a good impression as wags and wits studied their Aesop, and made a note of remembering the tales which they heard ('learned at the feast'), in case they didn't have an Aesop collection 'to pore over' at home. A large proportion of the surviving fables are not only jokes, but are even what we call today 'one-liners'. Aristophanes clearly thought of Aesop as primarily a humorist.

The popularity of Aesop is also shown by the fact that Plato records that Socrates decided to versify some of his fables while he was in jail awaiting execution (*Phaedo* 60b). The Platonic dialogues mention Aesop several times. Fable 196 is referred to in the dialogue *The First Alcibiades* (123a) in a very clever way. (This dialogue is one of the disputed dialogues of Plato, so that its authorship is not certain.)

But the deepest appreciation of Aesop in Greek times was shown by Aristotle and his school. Aristotle was a systematic collector of riddles, proverbs and folklore. He made a special study of riddles promulgated by the Delphic oracle, whose history he was keen to record. He probably collected Aesop fables in the way that he collected everything else, and farmed out their systemization to his pupils. Doubtless through the agency of his nephew Callisthenes, who accompanied Alexander on his military expeditions, Aristotle seems to have acquired the Assyrian *Book of Aḥiqar*, which contained fables, some of which were related to 'Aesop' fables. Aristotle's colleague, Theophrastus, published a book of this title (in Greek *Akicharos*), apparently a translation into Greek with his commentary (now completely lost). Theophrastus's pupil, Demetrius of Phalerum, then made a collection of Aesop fables – approximately a hundred of them – which became the standard collection for several centuries to come. If it were not for the efforts of Demetrius, most of the Aesop fables known to us today would certainly have been lost. He may well have compiled his edition of Aesop as well as his book, *Sayings of the Seven Wise Men*, from collected material in the library of Aristotle's Lyceum at Athens, which would have been his 'local university library', as he was a student there for a considerable time.

Aristotle's pupil, Chamaileon, also well known to Demetrius, made a study of the so-called 'Libyan Stories', which Aristotle says in his *Rhetoric* (II, 20, 1392b) was another collection of fables, since he there speaks of such material useful in making speeches as 'the fables of Aesop, or those from Libya'. Several of these 'Libyan Stories' appear to survive in our present Aesop collection, as we shall note in a moment. Chamaileon, in a lost work (the fragments of which were not collected by Wehrli but only by Alberta Lorenzoni in *Museum Criticum* (13/14 (1978–9) 321 ff.)), identified the author of the 'Libyan Stories' as Kybissos or Kybisses. Chamaileon seems to have continued his discussion of fables from various lands by identifying a man named Thouris as the author of certain 'Sybaritic tales', which were also fables (these are the 'jests from Sybaris' mentioned by Aristophanes in *The Wasps*), and another man named Konnis as the author of some Cilician fables from Asia Minor. The author Theon, who appears to have drawn from Chamaileon, goes on to speak of fables coming also from Phrygia and Egypt. We must bear in mind that some or all of these fable collections may be represented in our present 'Aesop' collection.

Aristotle actually records earlier variants of two Aesop fables, Fable 19 in his *Meteorology* and Fable 124 in *The Parts of Animals* (see notes to these fables). And, in his *Rhetoric* (II, 20, 1393b24), he tells an interesting story of how Aesop, then living on the island of Samos, defended a popular leader being tried for his life before the Assembly by telling a fable about a fox crossing a river who was swept away by the current. The fox became stuck in a hole in the rocks, where, being afflicted by swarms of fleas, she asked a passing hedgehog who had expressed sympathy not to relieve her of them because 'These fleas are by this time full of me and not sucking much blood; if you take them away, others will come with fresh appetites and drink up all the blood I have left.' Aesop used this fable to say that his client was wealthy already and, if put to death, others would come along who would rob the treasury, whereas he didn't need to. Aristotle had spent a great deal of time studying the history of Samos, and it is highly likely that this story is accurate; it indicates that Aesop was a lawyer who pleaded before the Samian Assembly and, in doing so, used his own fables in the way orators would do for centuries to come. This particular fable is most probably genuine, but was later lost (and so is not in this collection).

B. E. Perry is one of the leading Aesop scholars, having published as much on the subject as anyone in the twentieth century, and it was his view that true Aesop fables were likely to be the ones with mythological elements. An example would be Fable 120, 'Zeus and the Men'. Such fables tend to combine strange myths of how or why something came to be as it is, together with an amusing twist. Others would be Fable 73, 'The North Wind and the Sun', Fable 121, 'Zeus and Apollo', Fable 123, 'Zeus and the Jar of Good Things' (which is related to the story of Pandora's Box), Fable 126, 'Zeus the Judge', Fable 210, 'The Lion, Prometheus and the Elephant', Fable 234, 'The Bees and Zeus', Fable 291, 'The Trodden-on Snake and Zeus', Fable 298, 'The Receiver of a Deposit of Money, and the God Horkos', Fable 319, 'Polemos and Hybris', Fable 322, 'Prometheus and Men'. Fable 124, 'Zeus, Prometheus, Athena and Momos' sometimes changed its cast of characters; it is also known as 'Poseidon, Zeus, Athena and Momos' in another version, and yet another version was recorded by Aristotle in *The Parts of Animals*, mentioned above.

Not only did the mythological identities of the gods shift and change, but Perry accurately detected a tendency for the fables to become 'de-mythologized' as time went on. A perfect example of what he means is Fable 19, which features 'the earth' swallowing the sea, but we know from Aristotle's *Meteorology* (III, 356b11) that in the original version it was Charybdis, not 'the earth', who swallowed the sea. As Greek culture evolved people became less devout and the old myths ceased to have any particular mystique. The fables thus tended to have their original mythological elements dropped, and neutral forces of nature substituted in their stead. In short, the fables became increasingly mundane and everyday, and lost much of their archaic quality. To detect these developments helps give us a feel for, among other things, how antique a particular fable might be, whether it might really be by Aesop or not and how debased a version we have in front of us.

Another aspect of the fables which Perry believed could help date them was a change in the usage of a word: *logos*. In the old days – prior to the Hellenistic period which dates from the reign of Alexander the Great – a fable tended to be called a *logos*. After that, the use of the word *logos* in that sense dropped out of fashion altogether. The word *mythos* was used instead. The 'morals' appearing at the end of many of the fables are of three types: some begin 'This *logos* shows that . . .', others 'This *mythos* shows that . . .' and a third type that begin in a different way, such as 'Thus . . .' Perry believed that the ones in the first category were all older than the ones in the second category, the former dating roughly prior to Alexander the Great, and the latter later in date in accordance with the change in the usage of the two words. This makes a great deal of sense and is probably correct.

In this translation we did not differentiate between the two, however, as we thought it would become tedious to have to have literally hundreds of occurrences of the Greek words. We simply say 'This fable shows that . . .' Anyone who is sufficiently interested in the relative dates of the fables to want to differentiate between the two categories can consult the Greek text of Chambry's edition (see 'A Note on the Text'). But we never translate 'This fable shows that . . .' unless it is either a *logos* or a *mythos*, and the fables without either can always be distinguished. As regards those, the thinking seems to be that most of them are later still, but, on the other hand, a few of them which are of an archaic nature may be the oldest of all. For the morals seem to have been added later than the fables to which they are attached, and the relative dates indicated by the morals are not the relative dates of the composition of the fables but of their *collection*.

Some remarks need to be made about the morals. It will readily appear to most readers that the morals are often silly and inferior in wit and interest to the fables themselves. Some of them are truly appalling, even idiotic. Because they were added later by collectors of the fables, we have separated them from the fables and print them in italics. Not all the fables have morals, but most do. (When there is none in our translation, they are missing in the text.) Occasionally one comes across a really literate and worthy moral, such as that appended to Fable 22: 'Thus it is that what skill denies us, chance often gives us freely.' Such morals were added in a more philosophical spirit. But the ones that commence 'This fable shows that . . .' can be taken as having been written by orators and rhetoricians who collected the fables for use in speeches and oratory. The morals were intended as guides to someone thumbing through the collection looking for an apt story for a particular use. For instance, Fable 77 'is aimed at people who pick arguments' and, regarding Fable 74, 'One could apply this fable to those who are exposed to disgrace . . .' As for Fable 120, 'This fable applies to a man of great stature but of small spirit.' Fable 185 'applies to the covetous', Fable 234 'is applicable to those who suffer as a result of their own envy'.

Sometimes the morals even refer to specific situations in assemblies or courts: for Fable 289 we are told '. . . in the city-states, people who interfere in the quarrels of the demagogues become, without suspecting it, the victims of both sides', and again for Fable 304 we are reminded that 'This fable shows that by meddling in affairs which one doesn't understand, not only does one gain nothing, but one also does oneself harm' – a suitable rebuke to a citizen who dares to speak against a policy when he has not taken part in public affairs. And Fable 301 is directed against 'men carried away by the strength of their passions [who] thoughtlessly undertake ventures . . .', to be used against the demagogues who, in a passion, urge a heedless policy. And someone speaking in the assembly who wanted to urge the appeasement of a threatening but dominant power could use Fable 121, the moral to which identifies it as expressing the sentiment: '. . . by struggling with rivals stronger than ourselves whom we cannot possibly overtake, we expose ourselves to mockery'.

We probably owe the preservation of the fables to their utilitarian use by orators and rhetoricians, so we must not begrudge them their morals. In fact, as long as one realizes the nature and origin of the morals, they develop a kind of kitsch fascination in themselves, like taking an interest in ornamental teapots.

The fables themselves are far from the sugary children's stories that many might imagine them to be. Most of those children's editions of Aesop are carefully selected and so heavily rewritten and artificially expanded that they have only a tenuous connection with Aesop. At least one hundred of the most interesting fables, namely the weirder mythological ones, appear never to have been translated into English at all, so that the fables as a whole have thus been 'purged' or 'whitewashed' and given a false image until now of a 'classic'. But perhaps that is the reason: a classic is something which is arrived at by consensus, and the weirder of the Aesop fables might have destroyed that consensus pretty quickly if anybody but a Greek scholar had ever been able to read them. For the fables are not the pretty purveyors of Victorian morals that we have been led to believe. They are instead savage, coarse, brutal, lacking in all mercy or compassion, and lacking also in any political system other than absolute monarchy. With one exception the kings are tyrants, and the women who appear include a young wife who scratches and claws at her (evidently brutal) husband's face, and one who is really an animal disguised as a human who pounces on a mouse to eat it.

This is largely a world of brutal, heartless men – and of cunning, of wickedness, of murder, of treachery and deceit, of laughter at the misfortune of others, of mockery and contempt. It is also a world of savage humour, of deft wit, of clever wordplay, of one-upmanship, of 'I told you so!' So stark is the world of Aesop that it calls to mind two reflections: first, women were relegated to such obscurity and powerlessness that they were unable to influence the actions of men or ameliorate them, and were essentially slaves. (We know from an analysis of surviving legal speeches that in classical Athens a woman who was an heiress could be seized from her husband and children, forcibly divorced and married to a distant male relative whom she didn't even know simply because she was the legal conduit through which property flowed within her father's family, and a family property owner must be male.) Second, there seems to have been no general public consensus that compassion towards one's fellow human beings had anything particularly to recommend it.

The latter observation is an important one, for we probably tend to underestimate the ethical transformation of Western culture which came about as a result of Christianity. In the West today there is also much brutality, violence and corruption, but among all of that there is also a widespread public consensus that it is a good thing to be kind to children, to care about the unfortunate, to help one's neighbour, to assist the elderly across busy streets and to come to the assistance of someone in distress who may be drowning or being murdered in the street. But these attitudes seem to have been absent in ancient Greece except in the case of occasional individuals. The underlying ethos of the world of Aesop is 'you're on your own, and if you meet people who are unfortunate, kick them while they are down'. The law of the jungle seemed to prevail in the world of men as well as of animals for Aesop. Perhaps that is why animal stories were so appropriate.

The Aesop fables provide fascinating glimpses of ordinary life in ancient Greece. Details emerge of objects of daily use, such as wigs and dog collars, which are occasionally surprising. Through the fables one gets inside people's homes, learns what mice liked to eat – and hence what was in the larder – how pets were treated, how sons were spoilt, how superstitious everyone was, how merchants and tradesmen thought and acted, how a farmer could take it into his head to set up as a merchant trader and set out to sea with a small cargo of goods, how frequent disastrous shipwrecks were, how mistreated the donkeys were, how a miser would bury his gold, how a master would buy a new slave, how one staved off mockery by quick repartee. Such insights enable us to have the kind of understanding of ancient Greek life which does not come from reading Plato or Thucydides. Here we are face to face with peasants, tradesmen and ordinary folk, not mixing with the educated classes. Coarse peasant humour is found throughout the Aesop material, and some of the jokes would not be out of place in rough country localities round the globe at the present day.

The fables are essentially a joke collection. They are an ancient joke book in the same sense that Artemidorus's *Oneirokritika* (late second century AD) is an ancient dream book. These collections were meant to be thumbed through and consulted for relevant items as occasion demanded. They were reference books of material intended for use.

The combination of humour and barbarism so characteristic of the Aesop fables may have alienated many classical scholars. Certainly there are any number of scholars of a snobbish disposition who would think it beneath them to concern themselves with coarse peasant jokes and the doings of the man-about-the-market-place. Such factors must be involved in the strange lack of attention given to the Aesop fables by classical scholars, and the lack of a previous English translation of the entire corpus. Nor is any Greek text of them in print to my knowledge. Instead of issuing a volume or even part of a volume of Aesop, the Loeb Library published in 1965 a volume entitled *Babrius and Phaedrus* by B. E. Perry, the Aesop scholar. Babrius and Phaedrus are literati who took the Aesop fables and expanded and adapted them in verse in the first century AD. Why should they be given such attention, with carefully edited text and translation, when the originals are largely ignored? Babrius and Phaedrus are second- or third-rate adapters and of little appeal or interest in themselves. At the end of the *Babrius and Phaedrus* volume is a very lengthy appendix by Perry entitled 'An Analytical Survey of Greek and Latin Fables in the Aesopic Tradition'. This section does not include mention of all the fables to be found in Chambry, nor is its information always reliable.

We have taken great pains to get the identities of the animals and plants right because important points are involved. We are not merely being pedantic by insisting on calling a chough a chough. Choughs (sea-crows), now nearly extinct in Britain, were so common in ancient Greece that beggars took them around with them as many in London take mongrel dogs today, and 'to chough' in Greek meant 'to beg'.

Precision in the terminology also reveals facts such as that household pets in ancient Greece were not cats but domesticated polecats, or house-ferrets (galē); see Fables 76, 77 and 251. Only Fables 12, 13 and 14 of our collection actually mention cats (ailouros); in the case of Fable 14, about the cat doctor, the identity of the animal was probably changed when the fable was added to a collection. Cats came to Greece from Egypt, but until the Hellenistic period after Alexander the Great, they were rare or absent from Greek households. The famous fable (Fable 76) of the cat who was changed into a girl by Aphrodite is thus not about a cat at all.

Translating the fables was full of perils, and there were a few words which were not in Liddell and Scott's Lexicon. And with unusual words like diarragentos (Fable 193, 'ruptured', for a seagull's gullet), the Aesop reference is not given by them while a Babrius reference (his Fable 38, 'burst', for woodmen bursting a pine trunk with an axe) was (although it has disappeared from the 1996 edition), thus perhaps one more indication of the disregard shown to Aesop by most classical scholars over the years.

By virtue of our enforced familiarity with the Aesop fables, a number of ideas and theories about them forced themselves upon us. We began to notice certain patterns and clusterings, which I should take a moment to mention. These are related to certain strange anomalies. To start with one of the latter first, we thought it bizarre to say the least that the wild ass was several times represented as going hunting with the lion for game, which they were then to divide between them. Certainly the obvious fact that wild asses do not eat meat had somehow been overlooked here. Then it began to impress itself upon us that the lion fables were very similar, somehow more satirical and political, than most of the other fables, and the fox tended to be a crafty courtier or vizier to the absolute monarch, the lion. And we began to suspect that there was in these particular fables an underlying intention to parody courts and monarchs. We had here a cluster of fables which really represented political satire of a wholly non-Greek kind, with a cast of characters alien to Greece, and where the fox was a substitute for the jackal. Few ancient Greeks had ever set eyes on a lion, unless they had seen the odd stone carvings of Naxian lions on the sacred island of Delos – which archaeologists like to point out are imagined, rather than observed, lions, inaccurately proportioned and looking like hungry hounds. If the Greeks couldn't even carve a lion statue properly for a sacred site, why were they so keen to have lions as characters in such a large number of their fables? What was really going on here?

The situation seemed even stranger in that the camel appeared more frequently in the fables, despite its non-existence in Greece, than the pig, which at least did live there. So why all these foreign elements? It became obvious that substantial numbers of the Aesop fables as we now have them are non-Greek in origin. And thus it was of particular interest to discover that Aristotle (as mentioned earlier) spoke in the same breath of Aesop fables and 'Libyan Stories'. For the 'Libyan Stories' would necessarily have included Libyan animals, and Libya was notoriously infested with lions and jackals, and had many camels. A significant number of the lion fables are probably therefore some of those very 'Libyan Stories' which have otherwise disappeared and left no trace. They certainly do not appear to be 'Greek Stories'.

Fable 145 has a camel, an elephant and an ape – but none of these were Greek animals. This fable thus has to be of foreign origin. It also includes the detail that elephants are frightened of piglets. No Greek could be expected to know that. It would be something familiar only to people who had elephants. But who had elephants? The Carthaginians were later to use elephants to cross the Alps so, once again, the finger points at Libya. Fable 147 features a dancing camel. Who in Greece had sufficient knowledge of camels to be able to write a humorous fable as a joke about how a camel walks? This again points at Libya.

On the other hand, a few of the fables seem to have Egyptian, as opposed to Libyan, elements. A clear example is Fable 4, which is actually a jumbled mixture of sacred Egyptian traditions (see its footnote). Another obvious Egyptian element in a fable occurs in Fable 137, where a bird-catcher is bitten by an asp (Egyptian cobra), which does not exist in Greece. (Of course, this might be Libyan.) What is not so certain is whether the Egyptians or the Libyans had bird-catchers who used birdlime. Such a bird-catcher is really a stock character for a Greek fable. But if a Greek had written this, surely he would have had the bird-catcher tread on an adder, since adders occur in various fables and are the poisonous snake of Greece. Again, some of the monkey fables are clearly non-Greek. Fable 304 describes a monkey sitting in a high tree observing some fishermen casting their net into a river. But this is most unlikely to have happened in Greece. And Fable 306, which concerns a monkey and a camel, is another unlikely story to emerge from the Greeks, who, in many cases, had seen neither animal (despite the urban Greeks sometimes keeping monkeys as pets).

There are thus many anomalies regarding the animals and even, sometimes, the plants, which only seem explicable on the basis of attributing foreign origins to a substantial number of the fables. And as we have seen earlier there were foreign fable collections circulating in ancient Greece, none of which appears to have survived. It makes sense that some of them were absorbed into the Aesop collections. We are encouraged in drawing this conclusion also by virtue of the fact that B. E. Perry, in his study of Demetrius of Phalerum's role in preserving the fables, discovered that his Aesop collection seems to have included less than a hundred fables, and he also demonstrated that several of those later dropped out of the picture and are not included in the text of Chambry. So, according to that kind of reasoning, it may well be that in excess of 250 non-Aesopic fables were added to the collection. A few of these may be very short, not particularly inspired, rhetorical exercises. But, certainly, there is plenty of room in the existing collection to accommodate a batch of 'Libyan Stories' and maybe some Egyptian, Cilician and other foreign fables as well. Fable 29, for example, is actually set on the bank of the Maeander River in Asia Minor and presupposes familiarity with the fact that the river's mouth is at Miletus.

Political satire seems to be prominent in some of the lion fables, as well as the curious role of the wild ass as friend of the lion. Anyone who reads over the fables in which the lion appears as a character will see that, in most cases, the whole nature of the fable seems rather different from most of the collection. A one-liner such as Fable 194 could easily be Greek, because it uses the lion only as a representative of strength, almost in an abstract sense. But Fables 37, 38, 39, 41, 195, 196, 198, 199, 205, 207, 208, 209, 212, 213, 269 and 270 all seem to come from the same source. These sixteen almost give the impression of being fragments or excerpts from some satirical book of non-Greek origin, a work of political satire of rather a high literary standard and biting wit. And the strange character of the wild ass may be a substitute for some other creature who was indeed carnivorous. One possibility is that the fox was originally a jackal and the wild ass was originally a hyena. Such transpositions of animals are known to have happened frequently with the fables. The lion, at least, was renowned in Greece and could be accepted as a character, but since neither jackal nor hyena exists in Greece, the jackal was changed into the familiar fox and the hyena became another wild creature which could run very fast – but with the disadvantage that it was vegetarian and would have no interest in going hunting with the lion and hoping for a share of the catch.

So much, then, for the possible origins of the fables now collected under the name of Aesop. As for the connections between those few fables in common with ones found in India, it seems that we will never know for certain in which direction the transmission took place. (The notes to several of the fables in this collection give details of their similarities.)

I am convinced that the fables gathered here are of great importance, both for a better understanding of our past and as studies of human nature. The idea of representing human types as animals has the advantage of a profound simplicity, but is not simplistic. Anyone reading through the whole collection should be inspired to form a resolution to show more mercy in the future! Too many of the beasts meet with violent ends. The pungent American description of life, 'It's a jungle out there!' could be taken as the motto of Aesop. The fables are certainly a wonderful source of wry humour, of gnomic utterances, of witty asides, of barbed epigrams. They are a delight – a rather horrifying delight at times – but then we have always laughed at people slipping on banana skins, so why not laugh at Aesop's fables?

Robert Temple
February 1997

A Note on the Text

The text used for this translation is that of Professor Émile Chambry, published in 1927: *Ésope Fables*, *Texte Établi et Traduit par Émile Chambry*, Collection des Universités de France, Paris, 1927. Chambry's edition contains 358 fables numbered consecutively from their alphabetical arrangement by Greek title. We have taken Chambry's text to represent the 'complete' fables of Aesop for the purposes of this volume, although every scholar would probably alter the text by taking away some and adding others according to his or her own personal choices. There are many fables, some ancient, some not so ancient, which are not included in Chambry's edition, but since we have no knowledge whether any fables are by Aesop or not (or, if he did write them, whether any survive), the 'complete fables of Aesop' is whatever the editor of its Greek text chooses to say it is. We have not entered into such disputes, nor have we included discussions of the textual history of the countless manuscripts of fable collections which exist, since that has been treated at length by others, such as B. E. Perry and Chambry himself. We mention these issues in the Introduction only in passing.

A previous Penguin edition of Aesop, a translation by S. A. Handford, contained only 182 fables, slightly more than half of the number which we publish here. In that translation, new titles were fabricated by the translator and numbers assigned at random. Until now it has not been possible to identify the Aesop fables in English unambiguously, but the numbering system now makes that possible. We have also been conscientious in attempting to render the titles accurately in English.

As for the various Victorian and Edwardian translations of Aesop, they were not only limited in their scope, inaccurate in their terminology and sentimental in their morals, but the famous 'translation' of Croxall was more than half written by the translator himself. In this volume, nothing has been added to the text and the only changes or liberties taken have been to render portions of narration in the form of dialogue, in a handful of instances, without distorting the meaning, and occasionally to render, say, Aphrodite as 'Aphrodite, goddess of love', to be helpful to readers.

Above all, care has been taken regarding the identities of the species of animals and plants, which no modern scholar known to us has translated correctly. We have also checked the botanical and zoological issues against Aristotle, Theophrastus and other authorities. We have included some key Greek terms in square brackets when we thought that such elucidations would be useful or necessary, such as, for instance, making clear when we translated 'Nature' that the Greek word concerned was indeed *physis*. Notes necessary for clarification are given at the end of the fable.

The Good Things and the Bad Things

The things brought by ill fortune, taking advantage of the feebleness of those brought by good fortune, pursued them closely. They went up to heaven and there asked Zeus to tell them how they should behave with regard to men. Zeus told them that they should present themselves to men not all together but only one at a time. And that is why the bad things, living near to men, assail them constantly, while the good things, who have to come down from the sky, only arrive at long intervals.

Thus we see how good fortune never reaches us quickly, while bad fortune strikes us every day.

NOTE: Zeus was King of the Gods to the Greeks, equivalent to Jupiter, or Jove, to the Romans. His name will recur frequently throughout the fables, and in particular as the ultimate authority towards whom various plants and animals turn to settle their disputes, in his role as chief arbiter of all that happens in heaven and on earth. It should be remembered that in many cases these appeals to Zeus are intended as a joke, as is true of this fable for instance. A very large proportion of the fables, perhaps more than half, are formulated as jokes, and nothing was thought quite so funny as some lowly or pathetic group of creatures 'appealing to Zeus'.

2

The Man Selling a Holy Statue

A man carved a wooden statue of the god Hermes and carried it to the market to offer it for sale. But no buyer came along. So the man took it into his head to attract a buyer by crying out that he was selling a god who would provide both goods and profits. A passer-by heard this and said to him:

'Ha! Well, friend, if he is so beneficent, why are you selling him instead of making use of his help yourself?'

The merchant replied:

'Oh, it isn't that. It's just that I need ready cash and the god is never in a hurry to render his services.'

This fable relates to base, self-seeking men who are not sustained by the gods.

3

The Eagle and the Fox

An eagle and a fox, having become friends, decided to live near one another and be neighbours. They believed that this proximity would strengthen their friendship. So the eagle flew up and established herself on a very high branch of a tree, where she made her nest. And the fox, creeping about among the bushes which were at the foot of the same tree, made her den there, depositing her babies right beneath the eagle.

But, one day when the fox was out looking for food, the eagle, who was very short of food too, swooped down to the bushes and took the fox cubs up to her nest and feasted on them with her own young.

When the fox returned, she was less distressed at the death of her little ones than she was driven mad by frustration at the impossibility of ever effectively avenging herself. For she, a land animal [*chersaia*], could never hope to pursue a winged bird. She had no option but to content herself, in her powerlessness and feebleness, with cursing her enemy from afar.

Now it was not long afterwards that the eagle did actually receive her punishment for her crime against her friend.

Some men were sacrificing a goat in the countryside and the eagle swooped down on the altar, carrying off some burning entrails, which she took up to her nest. A strong wind arose which blew the fire from the burning entrails into some old straw that was in the nest. The eaglets were singed and, as they were not yet able to fly, when they leaped from the nest they fell to the ground. The fox rushed up and devoured them all in front of the eagle's eyes.

This story shows that if you betray friendship, you may evade the vengeance of those whom you wrong if they are weak, but ultimately you cannot escape the vengeance of heaven.

NOTE: This fable is told in verse by the poet Archilochus (eighth or seventh century BC) and also referred to by Aristophanes in 414 BC in *The Birds* (651), where it is attributed to Aesop.

4

The Eagle and the Scarab Beetle

An eagle was once pursuing a hare. This hare, seeing his position was hopeless, turned to the only creature whom fate offered for help: it was a scarab beetle. The hare begged the beetle to save him. The scarab beetle reassured him, and upon the eagle's approach the beetle beseeched him not to carry off the hare. But the eagle, disdaining his small size and insignificance, devoured the hare as the beetle looked on.

From that time, the scarab beetle, full of malice, never ceases to search out the places where the eagle builds her nest. And when the eggs are laid, the beetle gets into the nest, hoists himself up and rolls the eggs out of the nest so that they fall and break.

The eagle is consecrated to Zeus, and so the eagle appealed to Zeus to find her a safe sanctuary where she could raise her young. Zeus allowed her to lay her eggs in his lap. But the scarab beetle saw through this trick. He made a pellet of dung, took flight, and when he got above the lap of Zeus he let it fall. Zeus stood up to shake off the dung pellet, and the eggs were thrown to the ground without his thinking.

Since that time, it is said, eagles no longer nest during the season when the scarab beetles appear.

The fable teaches one not to despise anyone. One must say to oneself that there is no being so feeble that he is not capable one day of avenging an insult.

NOTE: This fable is a garbled distortion of sacred Egyptian mythology. In Egypt the sacred scarab beetle was envisaged as pushing the rising sun above the horizon, just as the real scarab beetle pushes the round dung pellet containing its own egg. The scarab thus symbolized self-generation. One of the eyes of the sacred hawk, Horus, was also the sun. In this fable the hawk has become an eagle. The rolling of eggs, the dung pellet, the sacred hawk/eagle and the chief of the gods, who has been given the Greek name of Zeus here, are all elements from Egyptian legend which have been jumbled up to make a fable. It is possible that this fable itself comes from Egypt, since there seems little reason for Egyptian religious tradition to form the basis of a native Greek fable. The scarab beetle appears also in Fables 149 and 241.

This particular fable is supposed, however, to have been told by Aesop to the hostile Delphians who were threatening to throw him from a cliff, according to the *Life of Aesop*, and also according to the playwright Aristophanes in his comedy *The Wasps* (1446 ff.). It may be, therefore, that Aesop was an eclectic gatherer of religious lore more interested in a good story than in any kind of accurate understanding of foreign doctrines, and hence the jumble of elements.

5

The Eagle, the Jackdaw and the Shepherd

An eagle, dropping suddenly from a high rock, carried off a lamb. A jackdaw saw this, was smitten by a sense of rivalry and determined to do the same. So, with a great deal of noise, he pounced upon a ram. But his claws merely got caught in the thick ringlets of the ram's fleece, and no matter how frantically he flapped his wings, he was unable to get free and take flight.

Finally the shepherd bestirred himself, hurried up to the jackdaw and got hold of him. He clipped the end of his wings and, when evening fell, he carried him back for his children. The children wanted to know what sort of bird this was. So the shepherd replied:

'As far as I can see, it's a jackdaw, but it would like us to think it's an eagle!'

Just so, to compete with the powerful is not only not worth the effort and labour lost, but also brings mockery and calamity upon us.

6

The Eagle with Clipped Wings
and the Fox

One day a man caught an eagle. He clipped its wings and released it into his farmyard to live with the poultry. The eagle hung his head in sorrow and refused to eat. One would have taken him for an imprisoned king.

But another man came along and bought the eagle. He lifted up the wing feathers and rubbed the place with myrrh so that they grew again. The eagle soared upwards into the air once more and spotted a hare. He seized the hare in his talons and offered it to the man as a gift.

A fox had seen all this and said to the eagle:

'You shouldn't give the hare to him. You should give it to your first master. The second master is naturally good. But you ought to give a present to the first one to deter him from catching you and clipping your wings again.'

Thus, one should generously repay the favours of one's benefactors and prudently keep out of the way of wicked people.

7

The Eagle Hit by an Arrow

An eagle had perched on the crest of a craggy rock to scan the ground below for hares. A man shot him with an arrow, which lodged in his flesh. The end of the arrow, feathered with eagle's feathers, stuck out of him and stared him in the face. Seeing it, he cried out:

'This is the crowning insult, to die because of the danger I myself presented!'

The pangs of suffering are made more poignant when we are beaten at our own game.

NOTE: We know from a fragment of the lost play, *Myrmidones*, by Aeschylus (525–456 BC) that this fable is not by Aesop but is instead one of the 'Libyan Stories', a rival collection of ancient fables mentioned by Aristotle, and for discussion of which see the Introduction.

8

The Nightingale and the Hawk

A nightingale, perched on a tall oak, was singing as usual when a hawk saw her. He was very hungry, so he swooped down upon her and seized her. Seeing herself about to die, the nightingale pleaded to the hawk to let her go, saying she was not a sizeable enough meal and would never fill the stomach of a hawk, and that if he were hungry he ought to find some bigger birds. But the hawk replied:

'I would certainly be foolish if I let a meal go which I already have in my talons to run after something else which I haven't yet seen.'

Men are foolish who, in hope of greater things, let those which they have in their grasp escape.

NOTE: A different fable of 'The Hawk and the Nightingale' is related by the poet Hesiod (circa 700 BC) in his *Works and Days* (201–10). In that fable the hawk has seized the nightingale and, as he carries her high up among the clouds, he tells the nightingale she should not cry out or resist his superior might, for: 'He is a fool who tries to withstand the stronger, for he does not get the mastery and suffers pain besides his shame.' This old fable clearly antedates the time of Aesop, and perhaps he or another wrote a fable with the same characters because they were familiar. Two points particularly noteworthy about the fable recounted by Hesiod are that it clearly preceded him and that it had a clear moral appended to it, showing that this practice of appending morals to animal fables was very ancient.

9

The Nightingale and the Swallow

The swallow urged the nightingale to take up residence under the roofs of men and live near them, as she herself did.

The nightingale replied:

'No, thank you. I have no desire to revive the memories of all my past misfortunes.'

Thus, some people afflicted by a stroke of bad luck wish to avoid the place where the misfortune occurred.

NOTE: The Greeks ate nightingales whereas they never ate swallows or house-martins; see Fable 349. However, the real point of this fable is a reference to a myth, known by everyone at Athens, about the daughters of the Athenian King Pandion, one of whom changed into a nightingale and the other into a swallow; see the note to Fable 350, which deals with the same story. The Greeks used the same word for house-martins and swallows, which were not distinguished in terminology, so that one must decide which is referred to by the context. In this case, the mythological reference is decisive.

10

The Athenian Debtor

In Athens, a debtor summoned by his creditor to repay his debt begged for more time because things were very difficult for him. Not being able to persuade his creditor, he led a sow, the only one he owned, and offered it for sale in front of him. A buyer came along and asked if the sow were fertile.

'Oh yes, she's fertile,' replied the debtor, 'extraordinarily so. During the time of the Eleusinian Mysteries she gives birth to females, and during the Panathēnaiac Festival she gives birth to males.'

The buyer was stunned on hearing this. The creditor added sarcastically:

'I shouldn't be surprised if I were you. Why, it's quite clear that this sow would also doubtless give birth to baby goats for the god Dionysius.'

This fable shows that people do not hesitate to pledge the impossible when they are desperate.

11

The Ethiopian

A man who bought an Ethiopian slave presumed that his [black] colour was due to neglect by his former owner. Taking him home, he set to work scrubbing him down with soap. He tried every method of washing which he knew, to try and whiten him. But he could not alter his colour. Indeed, he made himself ill with his exertions.

This fable shows that the nature of something is seen straightaway.

NOTE: The original version of this fable featured not an Ethiopian but an Indian. The older version is referred to by the satirist Lucian, for instance, who, in his Epigram 19, asks: 'Why do you wash in vain your Indian body? . . . You cannot shed sunlight on the dark night.' (See the Loeb Library *Greek Anthology* (428).) Themistius, in *Oration 23*, doubtless drawing upon the collection of Demetrius of Phalerum (see Introduction), also calls the man an Indian, as do several others, but the later writer of fables, Aphthonius, changes him to an Ethiopian. Thus do the fables mutate as they migrate from one writer to another.

12

The Cat and the Cock

A cat who had caught a cock wanted to give a plausible reason for devouring it. So she accused it of annoying people by crowing at night and disturbing their sleep.

The cock defended himself by saying that he did it to be helpful. For, if he woke people up, it was to summon them to their accustomed work.

Then the cat produced another grievance and accused the cock of insulting Nature by his relationship with his mother and sisters.

The cock replied that in this also he was serving his master's interests, since it was thanks to this that the chickens laid lots of eggs.

'Ah well!' cried the cat, 'I'm not going to go without food just because you can produce a lot of justifications!' And she ate the cock.

This fable shows that someone with a wicked nature who is determined to do wrong, when he cannot do so in the guise of a good man, does his evil deeds openly.

13

The Cat and the Mice

A house was infested with mice. A cat discovered this, went there and caught them one after the other and ate them. The mice, seeing themselves continually being caught, were forced back to their holes. Not wanting to wait endlessly for them to come out, the cat thought of a ruse to tempt them out. He climbed up on to a wooden peg and hung there, pretending to be dead. But one of the mice, poking his head out to have a look around, saw him and said:

'Hey, friend! Even if you're going to hang there pretending to be a sack, I'm certainly not going to come near you!'

This fable shows that sensible men, when they have put to the test the wickedness of certain people, are no longer taken in by their falseness.

14

The Cat and the Hens

A cat, learning that there were some sick chickens in a small farm, disguised himself as a doctor and, taking with him the tools of the trade, called on them. Arriving at the farm, he asked the chickens how they were.

'Fine,' they replied, 'as long as you get out of here.'

It is thus that sensible people are wise to the tricks of the wicked, despite all of their pretence at honesty.

15

The Goat and the Goatherd

One day, a goatherd was calling his goats back to their fold, but one of them loitered behind on some juicy pasture. The goatherd threw a stone at her, but he aimed so well that he broke a horn. Then he began to plead with the goat not to tell his master. But the goat replied:

'What's the use of keeping quiet about it? How can I hide it? It's there for all eyes to see, that my horn is broken.'

When the fault is evident it is impossible to conceal it.

16

The Goat and the Donkey

A man kept a goat and a donkey. The goat became jealous of the donkey, because it was so well fed. So she said to him:

'What with turning the millstone and all the burdens you carry, your life is just a torment without end.'

She advised him to pretend to have epilepsy and to fall into a hole in order to get some rest. The donkey followed her advice, fell down and was badly bruised all over. His master went to get the vet and asked him for a remedy for these injuries. The vet prescribed an infusion of goat's lung; this remedy would surely restore him to health. As a result, the man sacrificed the goat to cure the donkey.

Whosoever schemes against others owes his own misfortune to himself.

17

The Goatherd and the Wild Goats

A goatherd, having led his goats to pasture, noticed that they were mixing with some wild goats. And, when evening fell, he herded all of them into his cave together. The next day, a great storm raged. Not being able to lead them out to pasture as usual, he left them inside. To his own goats he gave only a handful of fodder, just enough to keep them from starving. But for the strangers, on the other hand, he increased the ration, with the intention of keeping them as well.

When the bad weather was almost over he let them all out to pasture. But, upon reaching the mountain, the wild goats ran away. As the goatherd shouted after them, accusing them of ingratitude for thus abandoning him after all the care he had taken of them, they turned round to reply:

'All the more reason for us to be suspicious. For if you treated us, mere newcomers, better than your old flock, it's quite clear that if some other goats came along you would then neglect us for them.'

This fable shows that one ought not to welcome the over-friendly advances of new acquaintances in preference to old friendship. We must remember that when we have become old friends they will strike up friendships with others, and those new friends will become their favourites.

18

The Ugly Slave Girl
and Aphrodite

A master was in love with an ugly and ill-natured slave girl. With the money that he gave her, she adorned herself with sparkling ornaments and rivalled her own mistress. She made continual sacrifices to Aphrodite, goddess of love, and beseeched her to make her beautiful. But Aphrodite appeared to the slave in a dream and said to her:

'I don't want to make you beautiful, because I am angry with this man for thinking that you already are.'

Thus, one must not become blinded by pride when one is enriched by shameful means, especially when one is of low birth and without beauty.

19

Aesop in a Dockyard

One day, Aesop the fable-teller, having some time to spare, went to a dockyard. The workmen teased him and provoked him to reply. So he said to them:

'In the beginning there was only chaos and water. But Zeus, wanting another element, the earth, to appear, required it to swallow the sea three times. The earth set to work and swallowed once, resulting in the mountains being formed. Then she swallowed the sea a second time, and she bore the plains. If she decides to swallow the sea the third time, you chaps will be without a job.'

This fable shows that if you try and mock those who are smarter than you are, the retort will be that much sharper.

NOTE: The fact that Aesop is described by the epithet *logopoios*, 'writer of fables', gives an approximate date for this fable, which was clearly not written by Aesop as it stands, since he is a character in it. *Logopoios*, which is the term used by Herodotus to describe Aesop (II, 134), is an early usage ending in the classic Athenian period. Already in Plato's time the term was beginning to be reapplied (see *Phaedrus* (257c) and *Euthydemus* (289d)). Also, the moral here uses the word *logos* for 'fable', rather than the term *mythos*, which was used during the later ascendancy of the rhetorical schools. (See the discussion in the Introduction for these two terms and the dating which arises from them.)

However, an earlier version of this very fable was actually recorded by Aristotle in his *Meteorology* (III, 356b11): 'The belief held by Democritus that the sea is decreasing in volume and that it will in the end disappear is like something out of Aesop's fables. For Aesop has a fable about Charybdis in which he says that she took one gulp of the sea and brought the mountains to view, a second one and the islands appeared, and that her last gulp will dry the sea up altogether. A fable like this was a suitable retort for Aesop to make when the ferryman annoyed him, but is hardly suitable for those who are seeking the truth.'

Thus we can see that the injection of Aesop as a character into the fable as we have it occurred at a later stage than Aristotle's time, that the original was a mythological fable just of the sort we believe Aesop to have composed himself, and that the process of 'de-mythologizing' the Aesop fables was well under way in the replacing of the mythical whirlpool Charybdis by 'earth' and setting the incident in a mundane shipyard.

20

The Two Cocks and the Eagle

Two cockerels were fighting over some hens. One triumphed and saw the other off. The defeated one then withdrew into a thicket where he hid himself. The victor fluttered up into the air and sat atop a high wall, where he began to crow with a loud voice.

Straight away an eagle fell upon him and carried him off. And, from then on, the cockerel hidden in the shadows possessed all the hens at his leisure.

This fable shows that the Lord resisteth the proud but giveth grace unto the humble.

NOTE: This moral, which calls the fable by the late term *mythos*, uses the term *Kyrios* (Lord) which, although it was used in inscriptions for Zeus and other Greek deities, is used as an epithet for both God and Jesus in the Christian gospels. S. A. Handford pointed out that the moral was the same as a passage in the New Testament Epistle to James (iv. 6). We have accordingly quoted the relevant words from the *King James Bible*. Handford believed that this moral was appended by a Christian, which is probably more likely than that the Epistle to James was quoting a popular maxim derived from an edition of Aesop. The moral is thus probably Byzantine in origin, and this fable does not come from the earliest collection since it is called a *mythos* rather than a *logos*; see Introduction and note to Fable 19.

21

The Cocks and the Partridge

A man who kept some cocks at his house, having found a partridge for sale privately, bought it and took it back home with him to feed it along with the cocks. But, as the cocks pecked it and pursued it, the partridge, with heavy heart, imagined that this rejection was because she was of a foreign race.

However, a little while later, having seen that the cocks fought among themselves as well and never stopped until they drew blood, she said to herself:

'I'm not going to complain at being attacked by these cocks any longer, because I see that they do not have any mercy on each other either.'

This fable shows that sensible men easily tolerate the outrages of their neighbours when they see that the latter do not even spare their parents.

22

The Fishermen and the Tunny-fish

Some fishermen who had gone fishing were very worried about the fact that they had caught nothing for a long time. Sitting in their boat, they wallowed in dejection. Just at that moment a tunny-fish, who was being chased, attempted to save himself and, with a loud thump, jumped accidentally into their boat. They seized him and took him back to their village where they sold him.

Thus it is that what skill denies us, chance often gives us freely.

23

The Fishermen Who Caught a Stone

Some fishermen were hauling in a large drag-net. As it was so heavy, they rejoiced and danced, imagining that the catch was a good one. But when they had pulled the drag-net to the bank, they found very few fish. It was mostly filled with stones and debris.

The fishermen were deeply upset, less because of what had happened than because of the disappointment to their heightened expectations.

But one of them, an old fellow, said to the others:

'Don't let's be depressed, friends. For it would seem that Joy has for its sister Affliction. And if we rejoice prematurely then we should expect its contrary to follow.'

Neither should we delude ourselves into always expecting the same success, considering how changeable life is. But we should tell ourselves that there is never such good weather that a storm might not follow.

24

The Fisherman Who Played the Flute

A fisherman who was a skilled flute-player made his way to the sea one day, taking with him both his flute and his nets. Taking up a position on a projecting rock, he started to play the flute, thinking that the fish would be attracted by the sweetness of his tune and would, of their own accord, jump out of the water to come to him.

But, after much effort, no fish had come, and so he put his flute aside. He then picked up his casting-net and threw it into the water, catching many fish. He took the fish out of the net and threw them on to the shore. When he saw them wriggle he cried out to them:

'You bloody fish, when I played the flute you wouldn't dance, but as soon as I stopped you started up!'

Some people always do things at the wrong moment.

NOTE: The *aulos* was not, strictly speaking, a flute. It was played by a mouthpiece and thus resembled more an oboe or a clarinet. The instrument is mentioned as early as the *Iliad*. It was made of reed, bone, wood, ivory or metal. This fable is recorded as a story told by the Persian Emperor Cyrus, in Herodotus (I, 141).

25

The Fisherman and
the Large and Small Fish

A fisherman drew in his net from the sea. He could catch big fish, which he spread out in the sun, but the small fish slipped through the mesh, escaping into the sea.

People of a mediocre fortune escape danger easily, but one rarely sees a man of great note escape when there is a disaster.

26

The Fisherman and the Picarel

A fisherman who had lowered his net into the sea pulled out a picarel. As it was very small, the picarel begged the fisherman not to take it yet, but to release it on account of its small size.

'But when I have grown,' it went on, 'and have become a big fish, then you can retake me. That way I will be more profitable for you.'

'But wait a minute!' replied the fisherman. 'I'd be a fool to let you go when I've got you in my hand just in hope of better things to come, no matter how large you might become!'

This fable shows that it is foolish to forfeit the profit that is in one's hand upon the excuse that it is too small.

NOTE: The picarel is a small marine fish of the family Maena, found in the eastern Atlantic and the Indian Oceans and the Mediterranean.

27

The Fisherman Who Beat the Water

A fisherman was fishing in a river. He had stretched his nets across and dammed the current from one bank to the other. Then, having attached a stone to the end of a flaxen rope [*kalos*], he beat the water with it, so that the fish would panic and throw themselves into the mesh of the net as they fled.

One of the locals from the vicinity saw him doing this and reproached him for disturbing the river and making them have to drink muddied water.

The fisherman replied:

'But if the river is not disturbed, I shall be forced to die of hunger.'

It is like this in a city-state; the demagogues thrive by throwing the state into discord.

28

The Halcyon

The halcyon is a bird who loves solitude and who lives constantly on the sea. It is said that to protect himself from men who might hunt him, he builds a nest in the rocks of the bank or shore.

Now, one day, a halcyon who was broody went up on to a promontory and, seeing a rock which projected out over the sea, made her nest there. But some time later, when she had gone in search of food, a squall blew up. The sea rose up under the force of the strong winds, rising as far as the nest, which was filled with water and the young birds were drowned.

When the halcyon returned and saw what had happened, she cried out:

'How unfortunate I am! I who distrusted the ambushes which can take place on the land and have taken shelter on the sea find that from the sea there is even greater treachery!'

It is thus that some men, through fear of their enemies, come to rely upon supposed friends who are even more dangerous to them than their enemies were.

NOTE: The halcyon was a mythical bird, although the name was sometimes applied to the kingfisher. In this fable, the nesting habits of a kingfisher – who nests in a bank – are described. But the mythical bird's habit of 'living on the water' is also assumed. Actual kingfishers flit across the water but continually perch on branches. This fable therefore mixes real and imaginary characteristics. For this reason, we have not simply translated the title as 'The Kingfisher'.

29

The Foxes on the Bank of the Maeander River

One day, some foxes assembled on the banks of the Maeander with the intention of quenching their thirst. But as the flowing waters roared past them they became fearful and got one another worked up about the dangers of the current, so that they did not dare approach it.

Then, one of the foxes thought he would show his superiority by mocking the others in a humiliating way about their cowardice. He made out that he was the bravest of them all. In order to prove his point, he jumped boldly into the rushing waters. As the current pulled him out towards the middle of the river, the others left on the bank called out to him:

'Wait! Don't abandon us! Come back and show us how we can find the place where we can drink from the river without danger!'

The fox who was being carried away by the current shouted back to them:

'I have an urgent message for the Oracle of Apollo at Miletus. I want to take it to him now! I'll show you the place when I get back.'

This story applies to those who, by boasting, put themselves in danger.

NOTE: The Maeander is a great river which winds its way through Asia Minor. The Oracle of Apollo at Miletus was at the mouth of the Maeander.

30

The Fox with a Swollen Stomach

A starving fox, having spotted a bit of bread and some meat that some shepherds had left inside the hollow of an oak tree, squeezed his way into the space and ate the food. But his stomach became swollen from so much food and he could not get out again. He began to wail and bemoan his lot.

Another fox passed by and heard these complaints. He went up to him and asked him what was wrong. When he learned what had happened, he said:

'Ah, well! Stay where you are until you become the size you were when you climbed in, and then you will be able to get out easily enough.'

This fable shows that time resolves difficulties.

31

The Fox and the Bramble

A fox who was jumping over a fence suddenly slipped. As he fell he grabbed a bramble to stop himself from falling. The thorns of the bramble stuck into his paws and made them bleed. Crying out in pain, the fox said:

'Alas! I turned to you for help and now I am worse off!'

The bramble replied:

'I'm afraid you've got it all wrong, friend. You tried to cling to me, but I'm the one who clings to everybody else!'

This fable shows that it is a foolish man who seeks help from those who, by their instincts, would rather do him harm.

32

The Fox and the Bunch of Grapes

A famished fox, seeing some bunches of grapes hanging [from a vine which had grown] in a tree, wanted to take some, but could not reach them. So he went away saying to himself:

'Those are unripe.'

Similarly, certain people, not being able to run their affairs well because of their inefficiency, blame the circumstances.

NOTE: This famous fable gave rise to the common English expression: 'Sour grapes.' *Omphakes* can mean 'sour', but it is more accurate to translate it as 'unripe', since the sourness was a result of the unripeness, and when Greeks used the word to describe grapes they were usually referring to their unripe state rather than to their taste. The same word was used to describe girls who had not yet reached sexual maturity.

33

The Fox and the Huge Serpent [Drakōn]

A fox, seeing a huge serpent asleep beneath a fig tree by the roadside, greatly envied him for his length. He wanted to equal him. He lay down beside him and elongated his own body until, overdoing it and stretching himself far too much, the silly animal split.

And thus it is with people who compete with those stronger than themselves: they rupture themselves in striving to compete.

NOTE: The serpent referred to here does not need to be a real creature, as the story is a joke. The normal word for 'snake' in Greece was *ophis*. Sometimes this word *drakōn* was used for a serpent; Homer used the two interchangeably. But apart from the mythological connotations of Greek dragons, such as the one supposed to have lived beneath the site of Delphi, the actual origin of the word seems to have been an attempt to give a name to the python or boa constrictor to differentiate it from normal snakes, hence the word is meant to suggest a very big snake such as that required by the fable. Normally in the fables, when a snake is referred to, it is called an *ophis*. Another point is that snakes do not normally sleep extended, but then this is only a story!

34

The Fox and the Woodcutter

A fox who was fleeing ahead of some hunters saw a woodcutter and pleaded with him to find a hiding-place. The woodcutter promised to hide him in his hut, and did so. Some moments later the huntsmen arrived and asked the woodcutter if he had seen a fox in the vicinity. He replied in words that he had not seen one go past, but by signalling with his hands he indicated where the fox was hidden. The huntsmen, however, took no notice of his gestures and simply took him at his word.

After they had gone, the fox emerged from the hut without saying anything. When the woodcutter reproached him for showing no gratitude for having saved him, the fox replied:

'I would thank you if your gestures and your conduct had agreed with your words.'

One could apply this fable to men who make protestations of virtue but who actually behave like rascals.

35

The Fox and the Crocodile

The fox and the crocodile were contesting their nobility. The crocodile stretched himself to his full length in illustration of his forebears and said that his forefathers had been all-round gymnasts.

'Oh, there's no need for you to tell me,' said the fox. 'Just from looking at your skin I can see that you have been doing gym exercises for so many years that you have quite cracked yourself.'

It is the same with men. Liars are caught out by their deeds.

NOTE: The crocodile actually boasts of his forefathers having held the position of *Gymnasiarch*. This was an elected post at Athens involving presiding over public liturgies in the gyms and paying the training-masters. In Sparta, the word was used simply to describe a training-master. Among the Greeks, the gyms were places of immense public importance, not just exercise or sports halls as they are today.

36

The Fox and the Dog

A fox slipped among a flock of sheep and took hold of one of the lambs. He pulled it from its mother's teat and made as if to caress it.

A sheepdog asked him:

'Just what do you think you are doing?'

The fox said:

'Oh, I'm just teasing and playing with it.'

'Well stop that at once,' cried the dog, 'or I'll show you what the caresses of a dog are like!'

This fable applies to the careless man and to the foolish thief.

37

The Fox and the Leopard

The fox and the leopard were having a beauty contest. The leopard boasted constantly about the marvellous variety of his coat.

The fox replied:

'How much more beautiful I am than you! For I am varied not merely in my body but in my soul!'

This fable shows that ornaments of the spirit are preferable to a beautiful body.

38

The Fox and the Monkey Elected King

The monkey, having danced in an assembly of the animals and earned their approval, was elected by them to be king. The fox was jealous. So, seeing a piece of meat one day in a snare, he led the monkey to it, saying that he had found a treasure. But rather than take it for himself, he had kept guard over it, as its possession was surely a prerogative of royalty. The fox then urged him to take it.

The monkey approached it, taking no care, and was caught in the trap. When he accused the fox of luring him into a trap, the fox replied:

'Monkey, you want to reign over all the animals, but look what a fool you are!'

It is thus that those who throw themselves into an enterprise without sufficient thought not only fail, but even become a laughing stock.

39

The Fox and the Monkey
Dispute Their Nobility

The fox and the monkey, travelling together, were disputing their nobility. Each of them enumerated his titles and distinctions along the way, until they arrived at a certain location. The monkey rolled his eyes and began to sigh. The fox asked him what was the matter. The monkey indicated a number of gravestones nearby and said:

'Ah, it is so difficult not to weep upon seeing these monuments to the slaves and freedmen of my forefathers!'

'Oh?' asked the fox, archly. 'Well, you may lie as much as you please, for none of them can arise to contradict you!'

It is thus with men. Liars never boast more than when there is no one about to contradict them.

40

The Fox and the Billy-Goat

A fox, having fallen into a well, was faced with the prospect of being stuck there. But then a billy-goat came along to that same well because he was thirsty and saw the fox. He asked him if the water was good.

The fox decided to put a brave face on it and gave a tremendous speech about how wonderful the water was down there, so very excellent. So the billy-goat climbed down the well, thinking only of his thirst. When he had had a good drink, he asked the fox what he thought was the best way to get back up again.

The fox said:

'Well, I have a very good way to do that. Of course, it will mean our working together. If you just push your front feet up against the wall and hold your horns up in the air as high as you can, I will climb up on to them, get out, and then I can pull you up behind me.'

The billy-goat willingly consented to this idea, and the fox briskly clambered up the legs, the shoulders, and finally the horns of his companion. He found himself at the mouth of the well, pulled himself out, and immediately scampered off. The billy-goat shouted after him, reproaching him for breaking their agreement of mutual assistance. The fox came back to the top of the well and shouted down to the billy-goat:

'Ha! If you had as many brains as you have hairs on your chin, you wouldn't have got down there in the first place without thinking of how you were going to get out again.'

It is thus that sensible men should not undertake any action without having first examined the end result.

41

The Fox with the Cropped Tail

A fox, having had his tail cut by a trap, was so ashamed that he judged his life impossible. So, resolving to urge the other foxes to shorten their tails in the same way in order that he could hide his personal infirmity in a communal mutilation, he assembled them all together. He advised them to cut their tails, saying that full tails were not only ugly but were a useless extra weight, and an obsolete appendage.

But one of the other foxes, acting as a spokesman, said:

'Hey, friend! If it wasn't in your own interest you wouldn't be giving us this advice!'

This fable concerns those who give advice not out of kindness but through self-interest.

42

The Fox Who Had Never Seen a Lion

There was a fox who had never seen a lion. But one day he happened to meet one of these beasts face to face. On this first occasion he was so terrified that he felt he would die of fear. He encountered him again, and this time he was also frightened, but not so much as the first time. But on the third occasion when he saw him, he actually plucked up the courage to approach him and began to chat.

This fable shows that familiarity soothes our fears.

43

The Fox and the Monster Mask

A fox, having crept into an actor's house, rummaged through his wardrobe and found, among other things, a large, beautifully fashioned mask of a monster. He held it in his paws and exclaimed: 'Ah! What a head! But it hasn't got a brain!'

This fable refers to men who have magnificent bodies but poor judgement.

44

The Two Men Who Quarrelled about the Gods

Two men were quarrelling about whether the god Theseus or the god Herakles was the greater. But the two gods, losing their tempers with them, revenged themselves each on the country of the other.

The quarrels of underlings incite their masters to be angry with them.

NOTE: Theseus and Herakles/Hercules were deified heroes rather than full-rank gods, but at the popular level they made do as gods, a phenomenon somewhat similar to the status of saints in Catholicism as intercessors who are meant to be 'more accessible' to the common man.

45

The Murderer

A man who had committed a murder was being pursued by the parents of his victim. Arriving at the edge of the Nile, he came face to face with a wolf. He was so scared that he climbed up into a tree at the waterside, where he hid himself. But there he caught sight of a huge serpent [*drakonta*], which was slithering its way towards him. So he dropped down into the river. But in the river a crocodile ate him up.

This fable shows that criminals pursued by the gods are not safe in any element, whether earth, air or water.

46

The Man Who Promised the Impossible

A poor man was very ill, and not expected to live. As the doctors were about to give up hope for him, he appealed to the gods, promising to offer up to them a hecatomb and to consecrate to them some votive offerings if he recovered.

The man's wife, who was at his side, asked him:

'And where are you going to get the money to pay for all that?'

The man told her:

'Do you think I might get better so that the gods can call me to account?'

This fable shows that men readily make promises which in reality they have no intention of keeping.

NOTE: A hecatomb was, literally, a hundred oxen, though in practice it was often fewer. A hecatomb was only offered on the occasion of a great public sacrifice by an army or an entire city.

47

The Coward and the Ravens

A cowardly man set out to go to war. But, having heard the croak of some ravens, he lay down his arms and froze stock still. After a while he picked up his arms and again began to march. But the ravens croaked again. He stopped and then he said to them:

'You can croak as loud as you like, but you aren't going to make a meal of me.'

This fable aims at those who are excessively timid.

48

The Man Bitten by an Ant, and Hermes

One day, a sailing ship sank to the bottom of the sea with all its passengers. A man who was a witness of the shipwreck claimed that the decrees of the gods were unjust, for to lose a single impious person they had also made the innocent perish.

There were a great many ants on the spot where he was standing. As he was saying this, it happened that one of them bit him. In order to kill it, he crushed them all.

Then Hermes appeared to him, and struck him with his wand [*rhabdos*], saying:

'And now do you not admit that the gods judge men in the same way you judge the ants?'

Don't blaspheme against the gods. When misfortune befalls you, examine your own faults.

49

The Husband and the Troublesome Wife

A man had a wife who was extremely rude to all the servants of the house. He wanted to know if she would behave the same towards his father's staff, and he sent her to visit his paternal home under a pretext. When she returned some days later, he asked her how the servants had received her.

'The herdsmen and the shepherds scowled at me,' she said.

The husband replied:

'Well, woman! If you weren't welcomed by the servants who take the herds out at dawn and don't return until sunset, what about those you had to spend all day with?'

It is thus that the little things reveal the big things, and that the things which are visible reveal those which are hidden.

50

The Mischievous Man

A mischievous man bet someone that he could prove that the Oracle of Delphi was a fraud. On a date which he had agreed, he took a little sparrow in his hand and hid it under his cloak, and then made his way to the temple. There he faced the oracle and asked if the object which he held in his hand was living or lifeless. He wished, if the god replied 'lifeless', to show the living sparrow; if the god said 'living', to present the sparrow after having strangled it.

But the god, recognizing his false intentions, replied:

'Enough, man! For it depends on you whether what you are holding is dead or alive.'

This fable shows that the god defies all surprise.

NOTE: The god of the Oracle of Delphi was Apollo. It is ironical that this story of all stories should appear in a collection of Aesop's fables, since there was a tradition that Aesop, in the sixth century BC, was thrown from a cliff and murdered as a result of accusing the priests at Delphi of being frauds!

51

The Braggart

A man who practised the pentathlon, but whom his fellow-citizens continually reproached for his unmanliness, went off one day to foreign parts. After some time he returned, and he went around boasting of having accomplished many extraordinary feats in various countries, but above all of having made such a jump when he was in Rhodes that not even an athlete crowned at the Olympic Games could possibly equal it. And he added that he would produce as witnesses of his exploit people who had actually seen it, if ever they came to his country.

Then one of the bystanders spoke out:

'But if this is true, my friend, you have no need of witnesses. For here is Rhodes right here – make the jump.'

This fable shows that as long as one can prove something by doing, talk is superfluous.

52

The Middle-aged Man
and His Mistresses

A middle-aged man who was going grey had two mistresses, one young and the other old. Now she who was advanced in years had a sense of shame at having sexual intercourse with a lover younger than herself. And so she did not fail, each time that he came to her house, to pull out all of his black hairs.

The young mistress, on her part, recoiled from the idea of having an old lover, and so she pulled out his white hairs.

Thus it happened that, plucked in turn by the one and then the other, he became bald.

That which is ill-matched always gets into difficulties.

NOTE: A *hetaira* was a 'female companion', a courtesan or concubine, as opposed to a legal wife. The English word 'mistress' does not adequately convey the full social meaning if we wish to be precise about ancient Greek society. Similarly, the man is described as a *mesopolios*, a form of *mesaipolios*, which means 'half-grey' but is also the word used by association to mean 'middle-aged' in Greek.

53

The Shipwrecked Man

A rich Athenian was sailing with some other travellers. A violent tempest suddenly arose, and the boat capsized. Then, while the other passengers were trying to save themselves by swimming, the Athenian continually invoked the aid of the goddess Athena [patroness of his city], and promised offering after offering if only she would save him.

One of his shipwrecked companions, who swam beside him, said to him:

'Appeal to Athena by all means, but also move your arms!'

We also invoke the gods, but we mustn't forget to put in our own efforts to save ourselves. We count ourselves lucky if, in making our own efforts, we obtain the protection of the gods. But if we abandon ourselves to our fate, the daimons alone can save us.

NOTE: The daimons were semi-divine beings intermediate between men and the gods, who might come to the aid of men from time to time if whimsy took them, or they might even be persuaded by promises of offerings.

54

The Blind Man

A blind man was in the habit of recognizing by touch every creature which he held in his hands, saying what kind it was.

Then, one day, somebody handed him a wolf-cub. He felt it and was unsure:

'I don't know,' he said, 'if it be the young of a wolf or a fox, or one of the other animals of the same family. But what I do know is that it is not to be put among a flock of sheep.'

It is thus that a wicked nature is often recognized by its exterior.

55

The Cheat

A poor man, being very ill and getting worse, promised the gods to sacrifice to them one hundred oxen if they saved him from death. The gods, wishing to put him to the test, restored him to health very quickly. Soon he was up and out of bed.

But, as he didn't really have any oxen, he modelled one hundred of them out of tallow and burned them on an altar, saying:

'Receive my votive offering, oh gods!'

But the gods, wanting to trick him in their turn, sent him a dream saying that if he would go to the seashore it would result in one thousand Athenian drachmas for him. Unable to contain his joy, he ran to the beach, where he came across some pirates who took him away and sold him into slavery. And they did indeed obtain one thousand Athenian drachmas for him.

This fable is well applied to a liar.

56

The Charcoal Burner
and the Fuller

A charcoal burner who carried on his trade in a certain house noticed that a fuller had established himself nearby. So he went to see him and urged him to come and live with him. He said they were so close that they could live with much less expense if they shared a single dwelling.

But the fuller replied:

'That is out of the question! For whatever I will clean you will blacken with soot.'

This fable shows that one cannot unite dissimilar natures.

57

The Men and Zeus

They say that the animals were made first, that God [*Zeus*] granted to some strength, to others speed and to others wings. But that man remained naked, and said:

'Me alone you have left without favour.'

Zeus replied:

'You have not taken notice of the gift I have granted you. And yet you have the most: for you have got the power of speech, which is mighty with the gods and with men. It is mightier than the powerful, swifter than the fastest.'

And then, recognizing the gift of God, man went on his way, in reverence and gratitude.

All men have been favoured by God, who has given them language; but certain of them are indifferent to such a gift, and prefer to envy the animals who are devoid of both feelings and speech.

58

The Man and the Fox

There was a man who had a grudge against a fox, for the fox had caused him some damage. He managed to seize it, and in order to take his full revenge, he tied a rope which had been dipped in oil to his tail. He set fire to the rope and let him go. But, prompted by some god, the fox ran into the man's fields and set fire to all of his crops, as it was harvest time. The man ran after him helplessly, lamenting his lost crops.

One must be lenient and not allow oneself to be carried away uncontrollably, for it often happens that people easily angered cause even greater harm to themselves than to those they wish to injure and increase the problems they had already.

59

The Man and the Lion
Travelling Together

A man and a lion were travelling along together one day when they began to argue about which of them was the stronger. Just then they passed a stone statue representing a man strangling a lion.

'There, you see, we are stronger than you,' said the man, pointing it out to the lion.

But the lion smiled and replied:

'If lions could make statues, you would see plenty of men under the paws of lions.'

Many people boast of how brave and fearless they are, but when put to the test are exposed as frauds.

60

The Man and the Satyr

It is said that once a man entered into a friendship with a satyr. Winter had come and the cold weather with it, so the man raised his hands to his mouth and blew upon them. The satyr asked him why he did that. The man replied that he was warming his hands because of the cold.

Then they were served a meal. As the food was very hot, the man took it in small portions, raised them to his mouth, and blew on them. The satyr again asked him why he acted thus. The man replied that it cooled his meal because it was too hot.

'Oh well, friend,' said the satyr, 'I give up on your friendship, because you blow hot and cold with the same mouth.'

We conclude that we should shun friendship with those whose character is ambiguous.

61

The Man Who Shattered
a Statue of a God

A man had a wooden statue of a god, and he beseeched it to do something to help him in his poverty. But his misery only increased and his poverty became worse, so that he became angry with the statue and, taking the god by the leg, he smashed it against the wall. The head of the god, suddenly broken open, poured forth a hoard of gold. The man scooped it up and cried out:

'You have a very contrary spirit! You are very ungrateful! For when I honoured you, you didn't help me at all, but now that I have smashed you to pieces, you respond by showering me with gifts.'

This fable shows that one gains nothing by respecting a bad man, and one gets more out of him by striking him.

62

The Man Who Found
a Golden Lion

A timorous miser came across the statue of a lion made of pure gold, but did not dare to take it. He said:

'Oh dear, oh dear! I don't know what will come of this strange bit of luck! I'm absolutely terrified. I'm torn between my love of riches and my cowardly nature. For is this sheer chance? Surely some god or spirit has made this golden lion and left it here for me to find? I'm torn in two. I love the gold but fear the image of the gold. Desire says, "Take it!" . . . but my fearful nature says: "Hold back!" Oh, fickle Fortune! You offer yourself but at the same time do not allow yourself to be taken. Oh golden treasure which gives no pleasure! Oh favour of a god which becomes a curse! And what if I took it? How would I use it? What on earth can I do? I know! I am going to go and fetch my servants and let them take this golden lion. I will watch from a safe distance while they do it.'

This story relates to rich men who don't dare either to touch their treasures or to put them to use.

63

The Bear and the Fox

A bear once boasted to a fox that he had a great love for mankind, since he made it a point never to eat a corpse.

The fox replied:

'I wish to heaven you would mangle the dead rather than the living!'

This fable unmasks the covetous who live in hypocrisy and vainglory.

64

The Ploughman and the Wolf

There was a ploughman who had just unharnessed his team of oxen and was leading them to the drinking-trough. Just then, a famished wolf who had been searching for food came across the plough and began straight away to lick the inner surfaces of the yoke, savouring the taste of oxen. Bit by bit, without his noticing, the wolf's neck went down into the yoke and got stuck there. Unable to free himself, the wolf dragged the plough into the furrow.

The ploughman returned and discovered the wolf caught in the plough. He said to him:

'Ah! You scoundrel-head, you! If only you would give up pillage and robbery and put yourself to work on the land!'

The wicked are not credible characters, and they really ought to do something useful once in a while.

65

The Astronomer

An astronomer was in the habit of going out every evening to look at the stars. Then, one night when he was in the suburbs absorbed in contemplating the sky, he accidentally fell into a well. A passer-by heard him moaning and calling out. When the man realized what had happened, he called down to him:

'Hey, you there! You are so keen to see what is up in the sky that you don't see what is down here on the ground!'

One could apply this fable to men who boast of doing wonders and who are incapable of carrying out the everyday things of life.

66

The Frogs Who Demanded a King

The frogs, annoyed with the anarchy in which they lived, sent a deputation to Zeus to ask him to give them a king. Zeus, seeing that they were but very simple creatures, threw a piece of wood into their marsh. The frogs were so alarmed by the sudden noise that they plunged into the depths of the bog. But when the piece of wood did not move, they clambered out again. They developed such a contempt for this new king that they jumped on his back and crouched there.

The frogs were deeply ashamed at having such a king, so they sent a second deputation to Zeus asking him to change their monarch. For the first was too passive and did nothing.

Zeus now became impatient with them and sent down a water-serpent [hydra] which seized them and ate them all up.

This fable teaches us that it is better to be ruled by passive, worthless men who bear no spitefulness than by productive but wicked ones.

NOTE: The *hydra* was actually a mythical creature as well as a water-serpent. The Lernaean Hydra of myth grew two heads for every one that was cut off. In this fable, an actual water-snake is not intended; the hearer of the fable is meant to imagine a monstrous bogey-hydra. Once again, the fable is intended as a joke. An encounter between a frog and a bogey-hydra occurs also in the epic parody *Battle of the Frogs and Mice* (82), attributed to Homer and published in *Hesiod, The Homeric Hymns and Homerica*, trans. Hugh G. Evelyn-White, Loeb Library Vol. 57, 1914, pp. 541–63, but probably written by Pigres of Caria circa 480 BC; see footnote to Fable 244.

67

The Neighbour Frogs

Two frogs were neighbours. One lived in a deep pond far from the track, while the other lived in a small, stagnant pool on the track. The one from the pond advised the other to come and live near her:

'You'll enjoy a much safer and better life here,' she said.

But the frog on the track would not be persuaded.

'Oh, it would be far too great an effort to uproot myself from the place that I know so well and which I have always called home,' she said.

And so it was that one day a chariot passed along the track and crushed her.

Thus it is with men: those who practise the lowest of trades die before turning to more honourable employment.

68

The Frogs in the Pond

There were once two frogs who lived in a pond. But, as it was a hot summer, the pond dried up and they went off to look for another one. In the course of their search they came across a very deep well. Upon seeing this, one of them said to the other:

'Friend, let's go down this well together.'

The other replied:

'But if the water in the well also dries up, how will we be able to get back up again?'

This fable shows that one ought not to undertake one's business too lightly.

69

The Frog Doctor and the Fox

One day, a frog in a marsh cried out to all the animals:

'I am a doctor and I know all the remedies!'

A fox, hearing this, called back:

'How could you save others when you can't even cure your own limp?'

This fable shows that if one isn't initiated into a science one ought not to instruct others.

70

The Oxen and the Axle

Some oxen were pulling a cart. As the axle creaked, they turned round and said to it:

'Hey, friend! We are the ones who carry all the burden and yet it is you who moans!'

Thus, one sees people who make out that they are exhausted, when it is others who have gone to the trouble.

71

The Three Oxen and the Lion

There were three oxen who always grazed together. A lion had his designs upon them and wanted to eat them, but he could never get at one of them because they were always together. So he set them against each other with slanderous talk and managed to get them separated, whereupon they were isolated and he was able to eat them one after the other.

If you really want to live in safety, keep close to your friends, retain your confidence in them and challenge your enemies.

NOTE: There was another version of this fable involving only two bulls, and in which the starving lion seeks the aid of a fox, who 'by crafty deceit sowed discord between the bulls so that they parted company, and thereafter the lion made easy prey of each bull separately'. This is the version preserved by the rhetorician Themistius (fourth century AD) and which is actually probably the original form of the fable. Related to the Themistian version of the fable is the frame-story of the 'Estrangement of Friends' section of the Indian *Pañcatantra*, where a friendship between a lion and a bull is broken up by a jackal (the Indian substitute for the fox). No one has ever worked out satisfactorily whether the Greeks borrowed fables from India or the Indians borrowed them from the Greeks after the time of Alexander the Great's invasion of north-west India. The Indian versions are always immensely elaborate and long-winded, whereas the Greek versions are generally short and simple. This probably points to a transmission eastwards, such that the simple fables became elaborated, which is generally how things happen, rather than the other way around.

72

The Ox-driver and Herakles

An ox-driver was bringing a wagon towards a town. The wagon fell down into a deep ravine. But instead of doing anything to get it out, the ox-driver stood without doing a thing, and merely invoked Herakles among all the gods whom he particularly honoured. Herakles appeared to him and said:

'Put your hand to the wheels, goad the oxen, and do not invoke the gods without making some effort yourself. Otherwise you will invoke them in vain.'

73

The North Wind and the Sun

The North Wind [*Boreas*] and the Sun had a contest of strength. They decided to allot the palm of victory to whichever of them could strip the clothes off a traveller.

The North Wind tried first. He blew violently. As the man clung on to his clothes, the North Wind attacked him with greater force. But the man, uncomfortable from the cold, put on more clothes. So, disheartened, the North Wind left him to the Sun.

The Sun now shone moderately, and the man removed his extra cloak [*himation*]. Then the Sun darted beams which were more scorching until the man, not being able to withstand the heat, took off his clothes and went to take a dip in a nearby river.

This fable shows that persuasion is often more effective than violence.

NOTE: This fable was cleverly utilized by the playwright Sophocles, according to Hieronymus of Rhodes in his lost work, *Historical Notes*, where he related a picaresque story of Sophocles seducing a young boy outside the city wall of Athens. They wrapped themselves in Sophocles's cape while they pursued their physical delights, and when they had consummated their act, the boy ran off with the playwright's cape, leaving him his own boyish cloak. This story led to the ridicule of Sophocles by the townsmen, and his rival Euripides boasted that he had consorted with the same boy without having to pay any such price. Sophocles then used the fable to form an epigram, claiming that it was the Sun God, and not the boy, who had stripped him of his cape, whereas the North Wind blew when Euripides seduced another man's wife. See Athenaeus, *Deipnosophistae* (xiii, 604).

74

The Cowherd and the Lion

A cowherd who was pasturing a herd of cattle lost a calf. He looked everywhere for it in the vicinity, but could not find it. So he made a vow to Zeus that if he ever managed to discover the thief, he would sacrifice a kid to the god in thanks.

Shortly after making this vow, he went into a wood where he saw a lion eating the lost calf. Terror-stricken, he raised his hands to the sky, crying out:

'Oh great Lord Zeus, a short time ago I made a vow to sacrifice a kid to you if I found the thief. But now I will sacrifice a bull if only I can escape from the thief's claws!'

One could apply this fable to those who are exposed to disgrace: in their difficulty, they desire to find a remedy, but once they've found it, they seek to evade their commitments.

75

The Linnet and the Bat

A linnet in a cage, hooked to an open window, sang during the night. A bat heard his voice from a distance and, coming near, asked him for what reason he chose to keep quiet by day and sing only at night.

The linnet said:

'I am not without motive. I make use of the night to do my singing because it was by singing during the day that I was caught. So since then I have grown wiser.'

The bat replied:

'It's a bit late now to be so much on your guard. It seems pointless. You should have thought of that before you were caught.'

This fable shows that when misfortune has come, regrets are useless.

NOTE: The Greek name for this bird in the cage is otherwise unknown in the whole of Greek literature – *bōtalis*. Liddell and Scott originally listed it in their *Lexicon* as *boutalis*, giving only the Aesop reference, and unhelpfully calling it 'a kind of nocturnal singing-bird', which, if they had read the fable, they would know was precisely the opposite of what it was! In the 1996 edition of the *Lexicon*, the nocturnal singing has been deleted, and we have no translation given at all, only the reference 'Aesop. 85'. *Akanthis* is given as either a goldfinch or a linnet, with the reference of 616b31 in Aristotle's *History of Animals* (which says the colouring of the *akanthis* is poor (i.e. dull), clearly ruling out both goldfinches and linnets) but unaware of the reference 592b30 which made the linnet an impossible choice (see below). At 593a1 Aristotle calls the goldfinch a *chrysomētris*, a translation accepted by Liddell and Scott, so that the *Lexicon* contradicts itself. Professor Chambry translates *bōtalis* as *serin*, 'canary', but adds a footnote saying that, as the word is otherwise unknown, that is only his guess. However, the canary is only a winter visitor to Greece and was much less common as a caged singing-bird than the linnet, which was the standard bird in Greece for this purpose and had the advantage that it sang throughout the year, which canaries do not.

The Greek terminology of the small birds was vague, and the name for the linnet is not really established by scholars. It has been suggested that it was the *akanthis*, but this cannot be so since Aristotle specifically states that the *akanthis* ate no insects (*History of Animals*, trans. David M. Balme, Harvard University Press, 1991, Loeb Library Vol. 439 (592b30)), whereas linnets do. There seems little doubt that the *bōtalis* is the bird called by Aristotle the *batis*. The word *batis* may be a contraction of *bōtalis*. Liddell and Scott list *batis* as 'a bird that frequents bushes, perhaps the stonechat', and give the single Aristotle reference (*History of Animals* (592b18)). The word *batis*, being otherwise unknown, is wisely left untranslated by David Balme in the Loeb Library *History of Animals*. However, it is described as a grub-eater (as linnets are, though they also eat copious seeds), along with four other birds, all of which are translated and identified.

Since Aristotle does not otherwise mention the linnet by any other name, and since there is an unidentified bird of its habits in his descriptions named *batis*, and since it is unthinkable that Aristotle would have omitted mention of the linnet in his thorough survey of birds, it seems reasonable to conclude that the *batis* is the linnet, by a process of elimination, and that *bōtalis* and *boutalis* are forms of the same name. If doubts are entertained about the linguistic possibilities of *batis* being a contraction of the longer word, we could always invoke a scribal error and suggest that *batis* in the Aristotle text is actually a misreading. It could even be *balios*, which means 'swift'. But such linguistic speculations are really unnecessary, since a linnet seems to answer the requirements of both the Aristotle passage and the Aesop fable, and there is, in any case, no other certain name for the linnet in Greek so it might as well be this one.

76

The House-ferret and Aphrodite

A house-ferret, having fallen in love with a handsome young man, begged Aphrodite, goddess of love, to change her into a human girl. The goddess took pity on this passion and changed her into a gracious young girl. The young man, when he saw her, fell in love with her and led her to his home. As they rested in the nuptial chamber [*thalamos*], Aphrodite, wanting to see if in changing body the house-ferret had also changed in character, released a mouse in the middle of the room. The house-ferret, forgetting her present condition, leapt up from the bed and chased the mouse in order to eat it. Then the indignant goddess changed her back to her former state.

Bad people who change their appearance do not change their character.

NOTE: Before cats came to Greece, or when they were still rare, the house-ferret, otherwise known as the domesticated polecat, was the chief household pet. The cat eventually usurped the polecat's position, so that people today no longer remember that polecats were once their intimate companions.

77

The House-ferret and the File

A house-ferret slipped into a blacksmith's workshop and began to lick the file that she found there. Now it happened that using her tongue thus, the blood flowed from it. But she was delighted, imagining that she had extracted something from the iron. And in the end she lost her tongue.

This fable is aimed at people who pick arguments with others, thereby doing harm to themselves.

78

The Old Man and Death

One day an old man, having chopped some wood, loaded it on to his back. He had a long journey to make. Worn out from the exertion, he laid down his load and called Death. Death appeared and asked him why he was summoning him.

The old man replied:

'For you to lift up my burden.'

This fable shows that all men are bound fast to life, however miserable their existence.

79

The Ploughman and the Eagle

A ploughman, finding an eagle in a net, was so taken by his beauty that he gave him his liberty and returned him to the wild. The eagle was not ungrateful to his benefactor; seeing him sitting at the foot of a wall that was in danger of collapse, he flew towards him and with his talons snatched off the headband which encircled his head. The man got up and began to chase him, and the eagle dropped the headband. The ploughman put the headband back on and retraced his steps, but he found that the wall had collapsed on the very spot where he had been sitting. He was well astonished to be thus repaid.

One good turn deserves another.

80

The Ploughman and the Dog

A ploughman was confined to his small farm due to bad weather, and he was unable to go out to find some food. So he first ate his sheep and, as the bad weather persisted, he next ate his goats. Eventually, as there was no respite, he turned to his oxen. Seeing this, the farm dogs said to one another:

'We had better get out of here. For if the master eats the oxen who work with him, we're next!'

This fable shows that you should be extra careful of people who are not afraid to harm those closest to them.

81

The Ploughman and the Snake Who Had Killed His Son

A snake slid up to the child of a ploughman and killed it. The plough-man, demented with grief, took an axe and went to keep watch near the snake's hole. He was ready to strike it the moment it came out. The snake poked his head out and the labourer hurled his axe but missed, and instead split a nearby rock in two. Having missed, he was in great fear that the snake would take his revenge on this attack by striking him with his fangs. So he attempted to appease it.

But the snake replied:

'Neither of us can pretend to any good feelings, neither I when I see the gouge you have made in the rock, nor you when you look at the tomb of your child.'

This fable shows that great hatred does not lend itself to reconciliation.

82

The Ploughman and the Frozen Snake

One winter, a ploughman, found a snake stiff with cold. He took pity on it, picked it up and put it under his shirt. When the snake had warmed up again against the man's chest, it reverted to its nature, struck out and killed its benefactor. When he realized that he was dying, the man bemoaned:

'I well deserve it, for taking pity on a wicked wretch.'

This fable shows that perversity of nature does not change under the influence of kindness.

83

The Farmer and His Children

A farmer who was on his deathbed wanted his children to acquire some experience of farming. He summoned them to him and said:

'My children, I am not long for this world. But, as for you, look for what I have hidden in my vineyard and you will find all.'

The children, imagining that their father had buried a treasure in some corner of his vineyard, hoed deeply all of the ground in it as soon as their father had died. They found no treasure. But the vineyard, so well tended, gave its fruit many times over.

This fable shows that, for men, work is the real treasure.

84

The Ploughman and Chance

A ploughman, while hoeing, chanced upon a hoard of gold in his field. So every day he crowned the image of Mother Earth with a garland, convinced that it was to her he owed this favour. But the Goddess of Chance [*Tychē*] appeared to him and said:

'Why, my friend, do you attribute to the Earth all the gifts I have made to you with the intention of making you rich? If times change and the gold passes to other hands, I am certain that it is me, Chance, who you will blame then.'

This fable shows that you must recognize the one who helps you, and return the favour.

85

The Ploughman and the Tree

Once there was a tree in the field of a ploughman which bore no fruit, and which served only as a roost for sparrows and humming cicadas. Seeing its sterility, the ploughman, went to cut it down with his axe and struck the initial blow. The cicadas and sparrows pleaded with him not to cut down their sanctuary, but to leave it for them so that they might chirp there and charm him with their music. Without paying any attention to them, he began hacking at the tree with his axe, giving a second and a third blow. But, having cut into the hollow of the tree, he found a swarm of bees and some honey. He tasted the honey and threw down his axe. From that moment on he honoured the tree as if it were sacred, and he took great care of it.

This proves that, by nature, men have less love and respect for justice than a desperate eagerness for gain.

86

The Ploughman's Quarrelsome Sons

A ploughman's sons were always quarrelling. He scolded them to no avail – his words did nothing to change their ways. So he decided to teach them a practical lesson. He asked them to bring him a load of firewood. As soon as they had done this he gave a bundle to each and told them to break it all up for him. But, in spite of all their efforts, they were unable to do so. The ploughman therefore undid the bundles and handed each of his sons a stick at a time. These they broke without any trouble.

'So!' said the father, 'you too, my children, if you stay bound together, can be invincible to your enemies. But if you are divided you will be easy to defeat.'

This fable shows that, as long as harmony is maintained, discord is easy to overcome.

87

The Old Woman and the Doctor

An old woman whose eyes were failing summoned a doctor for a certain fee. He went to her house and, each time, he treated her eyes with unguent. On each occasion while her eyes were thus shut, he stole her furniture piece by piece. When he had removed everything, the eye treatment came to an end and he demanded his agreed fee. The old woman refused to pay him so he took her before the judge. She then declared that she had indeed promised him a fee if he restored her sight, but since the doctor's course of treatment her condition was worse than before. For, she said, 'Previously I could see all the furniture at home, but now I can't see any of it.'

Thus it is that dishonest people, thinking only of their greed, furnish evidence of their own guilt.

88

The Wife and Her Drunken Husband

There was a woman whose husband was a drunkard. To get the better of him and his vice she devised a plan. She waited for the moment when her husband was so drunk that he was like a corpse, then she heaved him up over her shoulders, carried him to the cemetery and dumped him there. When she thought he had slept it off, she went back to the cemetery and knocked on the door of the vault.

'Who's that at the door?' the drunkard called out.

'It's me, who comes to bring food for the dead,' replied his wife mournfully.

'Don't bring me anything to eat, my good man. Bring me more to drink. You distress me by talking about food and not drink.'

The wife, beating her breast, cried out:

'Alas! How miserable I am! My plan has had no effect on you, husband! For not only are you not sober but you have become even worse. Your weakness has now become second nature to you.'

This fable shows that you shouldn't become habituated to a loose way of life, for there comes a time when habit forces itself upon you, whether you like it or not.

89

The Woman and Her Servants

A hard-working widow had several young servant girls whom she woke every dawn at cock's crow to set them to work. These servant girls, continually worn out from exhaustion, decided to kill the household's cockerel. For, in their eyes, it was he who caused their misery by waking their mistress before dawn. But, when they had carried out their design, they found that they had only increased their misery. For the mistress, to whom the cock no longer told the hour, made them get up even earlier in the dark to start work.

This fable shows that, for many people, it is their own devices that are the cause of their misery.

90

The Woman and the Hen

A widow had a hen which laid an egg every day. She imagined that if she gave the hen more barley it would lay twice a day. So she increased the hen's ration accordingly. But the hen became fat and wasn't even capable of laying one egg a day.

This fable shows that if, through greed, you look for more than you have, you lose even that which you do possess.

91

The Sorceress

A sorceress made a profession of supplying charms and spells for the appeasing of the anger of the gods. She was assiduous in her business and thus made a very comfortable living. But, envious of her success, someone accused her of making innovations in religion, and prosecuted her for it in court. Her accusers succeeded and had her condemned to death. As she was led away from the court, someone shouted to her:

'Hey, woman! You made such a profit from diverting the wrath of the gods! Why can't you divert the wrath of the people?'

This fable applies as well to a wandering seeress who promises wonders but shows herself incapable of ordinary things.

NOTE: Socrates was charged with making innovations in religion and condemned to death in Athens in 399 BC. Aristotle was similarly charged at Athens in 324 BC but had the good sense to leave the city to avoid execution.

92

The Heifer and the Ox

Seeing an ox at work in the fields, a heifer expressed sympathy to him about his punishment. But, at that moment, a solemn religious procession passed by, the ox was unyoked, and someone seized hold of the heifer and prepared to slaughter him as a religious sacrifice. At the sight of this the ox smiled and said:

'Oh, heifer, this is why you have had no work to do. For you were intended to be sacrificed.'

This fable shows that danger lies in wait for the idle.

93

The Cowardly Hunter and
the Woodcutter

A hunter was looking for the tracks of a lion. He asked a woodcutter if he had seen the footprints of a lion, and where the lair of the beast was.

'I will show you the lion himself,' said the woodcutter.

The hunter became deathly pale with fear and, his teeth chattering, said:

'It's only the trail I'm looking for and not the actual lion.'

Some people tend to be bold in words and cowardly in deeds.

94

The Young Pig and the Sheep

A young pig [*delphax*] mingled with a flock of sheep and was grazing with them. One day, the shepherd grabbed him and he began to kick and squeal. The sheep reprimanded him for squealing and said to the pig:

'We get caught by him constantly, and we don't make such a fuss.'

The pig replied:

'But when he gets hold of us – you and me – it's for different reasons. With you he wants your wool and your milk. But with me it's my flesh he's after.'

This fable shows that people who moan are justified in making a fuss if they are at risk of losing their lives rather than their money.

95

The Dolphins, the Whales and the Gudgeon

Some dolphins and some whales were engaged in battle. As the fight went on and became desperate, a gudgeon poked his head above the surface of the water and tried to reconcile them. But one of the dolphins retorted:

'It is less humiliating for us to fight to the death between ourselves than to have you for a mediator.'

Similarly, certain nobodies think they are somebody when they interfere in a public row.

NOTE: A gudgeon is a very small fish.

96

The Orator Demades

The orator Demades spoke one day to the people of Athens. As no one was taking much notice of what he was saying, someone asked if he could tell one of Aesop's fables. Agreeing to the request, he commenced thus:

'The goddess Demeter, the swallow and the eel all took the same route. They arrived at the edge of a river. Then the swallow flew up into the air and the eel dived into the water.'

At that point he stopped speaking.

'And Demeter?' someone asked. 'What did she do?'

'She got angry with you,' he replied, 'who are neglecting the affairs of the state to listen to the fables of Aesop.'

Thus men are unreasonable who neglect important things in preference to things which give them pleasure.

NOTE: Demades was an Athenian of the fourth century BC who commenced life as a sailor but became one of the leading orators of the Athenian Assembly and a great favourite of King Philip of Macedon. Later in his career he became corrupt and was convicted of taking political bribes. Cicero says the wittiest orators were the Athenians, but the wittiest of them was Demades. He was renowned for devastatingly quick-witted sarcasm, and would demolish a long and carefully crafted speech by Demosthenes with an impromptu aside, which made him a favourite of the populace. It is even probable that this little tale, which has been preserved among the Aesop fables – since it contains a part of a fable otherwise unknown – is an excerpt from a lost historical work, and represents a true incident from the life of Demades.

97

Diogenes and the Bald Man

Diogenes, the Cynic philosopher, was once insulted by a man who was bald. He replied:

'You have no right to insult me, God knows. On the contrary, I commend the good sense of the hairs which have left your wretched skull.'

NOTE: Diogenes, the fourth-century BC Athenian philosopher, was noted for his aggressive and acerbic remarks. He would trade insults with anybody. In all probability this fable preserves an actual remark he once made, praising the hairs that fled the head of an adversary who was bald. It is very much in character of the surly misanthrope, and the comment may have entered popular lore as a witty insult.

98

Diogenes on a Journey

Diogenes took a journey once and came to a stop when he reached the steep bank of a deeply flowing river, where his progress was obstructed. A local man, who was used to crossing the water at that place, saw that Diogenes was perplexed. So he went up to him, lifted him on to his shoulders and obligingly carried him to the other side.

Once they had reached the other side, Diogenes began reproaching himself for his poverty, which prevented him from showing his gratitude for this favour from his benefactor. While he was preoccupied with this dilemma, the local man saw another traveller who could not cross, ran up to him and began to carry him over as well.

Diogenes reproached him and said:

'I am not grateful for what you did for me, for I see it was not an act of judgement on your part but a manic compulsion which makes you do what you do.'

This fable shows that if you oblige insignificant people as well as people of merit, you expose yourself to being thought a man of no discernment.

NOTE: This story so accurately reflects the personality and opinions of Diogenes that it is, in all likelihood, based on some genuine comment or incident. It is the sort of imaginary example which Diogenes may have given when expounding an argument about the nature of gratitude, and may have been taken from some popular work about the philosophers. Diogenes was a disciple of Socrates; he lived in a barrel in Athens in the fourth century BC and founded the school of philosophy known as the Cynics.

99

The Oak Trees and Zeus

The oak trees complained to Zeus:

'We have lived our lives for nothing, grown up simply in order to be cut down. For, more than all the other trees, we are exposed to the brutal blows of the axe.'

Zeus replied to them:

'You are yourselves to blame. For, if you did not produce the handle of the axe, if you were not so useful to carpenters and in agriculture, the axe would never fell you.'

Certain people who are the authors of their own ills foolishly cast the blame on to the gods.

100

The Woodcutters and the Pine Tree

Some woodcutters were splitting a pine tree, and thanks to the wedges that they had made of its wood, they split it easily. And the pine tree said:

'I dread less the axe that cuts me than the wedges which came from me.'

It is easier to endure blows from strangers than it is from those nearest to you.

101

The Silver Fir Tree and the Bramble

The silver fir tree and the bramble were arguing together. The fir was boastful and said:

'I am beautiful, slender and tall. I serve to construct the decks of warships and merchant ships. How dare you compare yourself to me?'

The bramble replied:

'If you would but remember the axes and saws that cut you, you too would prefer the life of a bramble.'

You mustn't become too proud in life of your reputation, for the lives of the humble are without danger.

NOTE: There are translation problems with this fable, due to the fact that the Greek word *stegē* can mean both 'roof' and 'deck' (of a ship), and due to the fact that a temple is a *naos*, with Attic variants, and a warship is a *naus*, but with a declension varying wildly in different dialects and at different periods.

In the fable we have a genitive plural, *naōn*. Assuming that Chambry did not alter this reading in the preparation of his text, it could simply mean 'of temples'. But in certain declensions, such as one of the Doric declensions, it can mean 'of warships'. However, we have no way of knowing, without recourse to the manuscripts, whether the word might not have been the Attic *neōn*. Babrius rewrote this fable and spoke of the fir tree making a crossbeam or rafter (*melathron*) of a roof and the keel (*tropis*) of a ship. But these expressions are not found anywhere in the Aesop fable. S. A. Handford, in the earlier Penguin (Fable 140), spoke of 'temple roofs and ships'. Professor Chambry, whose edition seems to have been used by Handford, opted for the translation – in French, of course – of 'the roofs of temples and of ships'. But we have decided that ships don't really have roofs, and that silver fir is not the best choice for the massive roof beams of a temple. And, since the text goes on to mention merchant ships [*ploia*], it seems a translation of 'the decks of warships and merchant ships' makes more sense than 'the roofs of temples and merchant ships' and, furthermore, this is the kind of use of pine which seems more reasonable.

102

The Stag at the Spring and the Lion

A stag, oppressed by thirst, came to a spring to drink. After having a drink, he saw the shadowy figure of himself in the water. He much admired his fine antlers, their grandeur and extent. But he was discontented with his legs, which he thought looked thin and feeble. He remained there deep in reverie when suddenly a lion sprang out at him and chased him. The stag fled rapidly and ran a great distance, for the stag's advantage is his legs, whereas a lion's is his heart. As long as they were in open ground, the stag easily outdistanced the lion. But they entered a wooded area and the stag's antlers became entangled in the branches, bringing him to a halt so that he was caught by the lion.

As he was on the point of death, the stag said:

'How unfortunate I am! My feet, which I had denigrated, could have saved me, whereas my antlers, on which I prided myself, have caused my death!'

And thus, in dangerous situations it is often the friends whom we suspect who save us, while those on whom we rely betray us.

103

The Hind and the Vine

A hind, pursued by huntsmen, hid herself under some vines. Since these vines were a little overgrown, she thought that she was perfectly hidden and she began to nibble at the vine leaves. As the leaves rustled, the huntsmen, who had returned, thought rightly that they had their quarry hidden beneath the vines. They killed the hind with a chance arrow aimed into the leaves. She was pierced to the heart, and as she expired she spoke these words:

'I have only myself to blame; for I ought not to have damaged that which could have saved me.'

This fable shows that those who do harm to their benefactors are punished by God.

104

The Hind and the Lion
in a Cave

A hind was being pursued by some hunters and came to the entrance of a cave. Unknown to the hind, a lion was inside. She went inside to hide herself but was seized by the lion. As it killed her, she cried out:

'How ill-fated I am! In fleeing from men I have thrown myself into the grasp of a ferocious beast!'

Men, fearing a lesser danger, sometimes throw themselves into a greater one.

105

The Hind Afflicted by Deformity

A hind, rendered congenitally disabled by being born with only one eye, went to the seashore to browse, turning her good eye to the land to watch out for hunters and the blind eye towards the sea, from whence she expected no danger. But some boatmen-poachers were sailing along that part and they caught sight of her, adjusted their course, and mortally wounded her.

While rendering up her life she said to herself:

'Truly I am wretched; I was watching the land which I believed was full of danger and expected no harm from the sea, which has been much more perilous.'

It is thus that often our anticipation is mistaken: the things which seem troublesome to us turn to our advantage, and those things which we hold beneficial show themselves to be injurious.

106

The Kid on the Roof of the House, and the Wolf

A kid who had wandered on to the roof of a house saw a wolf pass by and he began to insult and jeer at it. The wolf replied:

'Hey, you there! It's not you who mock me but the place on which you are standing.'

This fable shows that often it is the place and the occasion which give one the daring to defy the powerful.

107

The Kid and the Wolf Who Played the Flute

A kid, lagging behind the rest of the flock, was being pursued by a wolf. He turned round and said to it:

'I know, wolf, that I am destined to be your meal; but so that I do not die without honour, play the flute and let me do a dance.'

While the wolf played and the kid danced, some hounds came running up at the din and gave chase to the wolf. The latter, turning to the kid, said:

'It is only what I deserve, for being a butcher it is not my job to be a piper.'

Thus, when one does something without considering the circumstances, one loses even that which is already within one's grasp.

108

Hermes and the Sculptor

Hermes, wishing to know how esteemed he was among men, betook himself, under the guise of a mortal, to the workshop of a sculptor. Espying a statue of Zeus, King of the Gods, he asked:

'How much?'

The sculptor replied:

'One drachma.'

Hermes smiled and asked:

'How much is the statue of Hera, Queen of the Gods?'

'It is more expensive,' was the reply.

Hermes then noticed a statue of himself. He presumed that, being both the messenger of Zeus and the god of profit-making, he was held in the highest esteem with men. He asked the price.

The sculptor responded:

'Oh, if you buy the first two, I'll throw that one in for free.'

Let this be a lesson to a vain man who has no consideration for others.

109

Hermes and the Earth

Zeus, King of the Gods, having fashioned the first man and the first woman, told Hermes to take them to Earth and show them where they should dig in order to grow their food. Hermes completed this mission, but Earth resisted the idea. Hermes insisted, and said that this was on the orders of Zeus.

'Oh well,' said Earth, 'let them dig as much as they like; they will pay with their sighs and with their tears.'

The fable fits those who borrow with ease and who pay with difficulty.

110

Hermes and Teiresias

Hermes wanted to put to the test the prophetic powers of the blind sage, Teiresias of Thebes, and to see if his practice of divination of the future by the signs of birds really worked. So he disguised himself as a mortal and stole Teiresias's cattle from the countryside and hid them. Then he returned to the house of Teiresias and told him that his cattle had disappeared.

Teiresias took Hermes with him to the outskirts of the city in order to observe some augury of the flights of birds relating to the theft.

'What bird do you see?' asked Teiresias.

Hermes said he saw an eagle which had just flown past from left to right.

'That doesn't concern us,' said Teiresias. 'Now what bird do you see?' he asked.

This time Hermes saw a sea-crow, or chough, perched on a tree. The chough raised its eyes to heaven, then leaned towards the sun and uttered its cry to him.

When he had this described to him, Teiresias commented:

'Ah, well! This chough swears by the earth and by the sky that it is up to you alone to return my cattle.'

One could apply this fable to a thief.

NOTE: Teiresias was a legendary blind prophet who often foretold the future by signs given by the flights of birds, which were described to him by his daughter, since he couldn't actually see them himself. He was famous all over Greece, though he lived before the time of Homer.

Hermes was the god of profit-making and trade, but also of thieves and knavery. This fable is only comprehensible in Greek; the wit involved depends upon puns and also a Greek begging tradition. Beggars used to carry a chough around, hence the Greek verb 'to chough' which means 'to collect or beg for the chough' and also 'to gather' – both referring to Hermes's act in stealing the cattle and also acting as a subtle insult to Hermes by calling him not a thief but a beggar. But also, the cry of the chough in Greek would be rendered *kaph* which is a form of *kap*, an abbreviation of the word for retail trader and knave or cheat. The bird's cry, therefore, served to identify Hermes to Teiresias, who was then able to recognize the true situation and make a clever reply. Most Greeks would have recognized all these double meanings and thought the fable very witty. It may not be a coincidence that in the ancient Babylonian *Epic of Gilgamesh*, *kappi* is an important bird call as well.

III

Hermes and the Artisans

Zeus, King of the Gods, charged Hermes to pour over all the artisans the poison of lies. Hermes pulverized it and, making an equal amount for everyone, he poured it over them. But when he got as far as the cobbler he still had plenty of the poison left, so he just took what remained in the mortar and poured it over him. And since then all artisans have been liars, but most of all the cobblers.

The fable applies to a man who adheres to falsehood.

112

The Chariot of Hermes
and the Arabs

One day, Hermes drove across the entire Earth a chariot filled with lies, villainy and fraud. And he distributed a small portion of his cargo in each country he visited. But when he arrived in the country of the Arabs, the chariot suddenly broke down. The Arabs believed he was carrying a precious cargo and so they stole the contents of his chariot. Hermes was then unable to carry on into the countries of other peoples.

More than all other people the Arabs are liars and cheats. Indeed, there is not even a word for 'truth' in their language.

NOTE: Arabia and the Arabs are mentioned in Greek as early as the fifth century BC, by the historian Herodotus. Since the Greeks had so little direct knowledge of the Arabs, it is strange that they should have had such a strong opinion about them. This fable may originate from a Greek settlement in Syria or Asia Minor or, more likely still, in Egypt, since contact with Arabs was not so unusual there. Arabs will find this fable offensive, and should avert their eyes.

113

The Eunuch and the Sacrificer

A eunuch consulted a sacrificer and begged him to make a sacrifice for him so that he could become a father.

The sacrificer told him:

'When I viewed the sacrifice, I prayed that you would become a father. But when I see you in person, you do not even appear to be a man.'

114

The Two Enemies

Two men who loathed each other were sailing in the same boat. One took up his position at the stern and the other at the prow. A storm blew up and the boat was on the point of sinking. The man at the stern asked the helmsman which part of the vessel would go down first. 'The prow,' he said. 'Then,' replied the man, 'death will no longer be sad for me, if I can see my enemy die first.'

This fable shows that many people are not in the least disturbed at the harm that befalls them, provided they can see their enemies' downfall first.

115

The Adder and the Fox

An adder was carried along on a clump of thorn shrubs by the current of a river. A fox who was passing by, seeing this, cried out to him:
'The worth of a vessel is its master!'

This concerns the bad man who surrenders himself to perverse ventures.

NOTE: The fox's ironical remark was doubtless a common saying at the time which he has cruelly applied to the pathetic adder being swept away. This kind of malicious humour was thought frightfully clever. This fable is thus a very good example of the continual preoccupation of the humour in the fables with 'scoring' at the expense of someone else's misfortune.

116

The Adder and the File

An adder slithered into a blacksmith's workshop and begged the gift of some alms from the tools. Having had something from some of them, she then went over to a file and begged it to give her something too.

'You're a fine one,' replied the file, 'believing that you can get something from me. For I am in the habit of taking from everyone, not giving.'

This fable goes to show that it is folly to expect to extract anything from the miserly.

117

The Adder and
the Water-snake (or Hydra)

An adder regularly went to drink at a spring. A water-snake [*hydra*] who lived there was annoyed that the adder was not content with his own territory but encroached on hers, and she wanted to stop him. As the feud festered, the two decided upon a battle plan. Whoever was victorious would have ownership of the land and the spring.

They fixed the day and the frogs, who hated the water-snake, looked for the adder and plucked up the courage to promise to take his side.

The battle began, and the adder struggled with the water-snake, while the frogs, unable to do anything more, made great croaks. The adder achieved the victory but he reproached them. He said they had promised to fight with him but during the battle, instead of coming to his aid, they did nothing but sing.

The frogs replied: 'Know well, friend, that we don't help with our arms and legs but only with our voices.'

This fable shows that when one needs physical assistance, helpful words serve no purpose.

118

Zeus and Shame

When Zeus fashioned man he gave him certain inclinations, but he forgot about shame. Not knowing how to introduce her, he ordered her to enter through the rectum. Shame baulked at this and was highly indignant. Finally, she said to Zeus:

'All right! I'll go in, but on the condition that Eros doesn't come in the same way; if he does, I will leave immediately.'

Ever since then, all homosexuals are without shame.

This fable shows that those who are prey to love lose all shame.

119

Zeus and the Fox

Zeus, King of the Gods, marvelling at the fox's intelligence and flexibility of spirit, conferred upon him the kingship of the beasts. However, he wanted to know whether, in changing his status, the fox had also changed his habit of covetousness. So, while the new King of the Animals was passing by in a palanquin, Zeus released a cockchafer beetle in front of his eyes. Unable to control himself upon seeing the cockchafer flit around his palanquin, the fox leaped out and, in defiance of all propriety and regal conduct, made attempts to catch it.

Zeus, indignant at this behaviour, placed him again in his former humble state.

This fable shows that those who come from nothing, though they may seem brilliant on the outside, do not change their inner nature.

120

Zeus and the Men

Having made men, Zeus entrusted Hermes with pouring over them some intelligence. Hermes, making equal quantities, poured for each man his portion. Thus it happened that the short men, covered by their portion, became sensible people, but the tall men, not being covered all over by the mixture, had less sense than the others.

This fable applies to a man of great stature but of small spirit.

121

Zeus and Apollo

Zeus and Apollo were competing at archery. When Apollo took up his bow and let fly his arrows, Zeus took a stride forward, covering the same distance as Apollo's arrow.

Similarly, by struggling with rivals stronger than ourselves whom we cannot possibly overtake, we expose ourselves to mockery.

122

Zeus and the Snake

When Zeus got married, all the animals brought him presents, each according to his means. The snake crawled up to him, a rose in his mouth. Upon seeing him, Zeus said:

'From all the others I accept these gifts, but from your mouth I absolutely refuse one.'

This fable shows that you should fear the favours of the wicked.

123

Zeus and the Jar of Good Things

Zeus shut up all good things in a huge wine jar [*pithos*], which he left in the hands of a man. This man was curious and wanted to know what was inside. So he prised open the lid and all the good things blew away, flying up to the gods.

Thus, hope alone remains with men, and promises them the good things which have fled.

124

Zeus, Prometheus, Athena and Momos

Zeus made a bull, Prometheus made a man and Athena made a house. They invited Momos to judge their handiwork. He was so jealous of it that he said that Zeus had made a mistake in not putting the bull's eyes on his horns so that he could see where he was butting. Likewise, Prometheus should have attached man's mind [*phrēn*] outside his body so that his wicked qualities were not hidden but could be there for all to see. As for Athena, he told her that she should put wheels on her house so that if an undesirable person moved in next door one could move away easily.

Zeus was so enraged by Momos's jealousy that he banished him from Olympus.

This fable shows that nothing is too perfect for criticism.

NOTE: By the time Babrius, in his Fable 59, got around to rewriting this fable in the first century AD, he changed things so that Poseidon made the bull, Zeus made man, but Athena still made the house. Babrius also changed it to say that the bull should have had his horns placed beneath his eyes so that he could see better where he struck. S. A. Handford, in the earlier Penguin (Fable 155), said the bull should have its eyes *in* his horns rather than *on* his horns. But the Greek of the fable says *epi tois kerasin*, and *epi* with the dative unquestionably means 'on' or 'upon', so that I suspect that Handford's version must have involved a misprint; he could not possibly really have intended 'in'.

Aristotle, in his zoological work *The Parts of Animals* (trans. A. L. Peck, 1961, Loeb Library Vol. 323 (3,2,663a)), refers to a variant of this fable which was well known in the fourth century BC, and he names Aesop as its author. However, in that earlier version, Momos 'finds fault with the bull for having his horns on the head, which is the weakest part of all, instead of on the shoulders'. Aristotle then proceeds to criticize Momos's suggestions. The later classical authors Lucian and Philostratus also allude to variants of this fable in which, again, two of the gods criticized by Momos were different. This minor god Momos, whose name is related to the word for 'blame' or 'complaint', was the god of satire, often represented in classical art as lifting a mask from his face. Sophocles wrote a lost satyr play entitled *Momos*. The variants of this fable are actually a chief source of our limited knowledge about Momos, who is otherwise insufficiently known.

125

Zeus and the Tortoise

Zeus entertained all the animals at his wedding feast. Only the tortoise was absent. Puzzled by his absence, Zeus asked her the next day:

'Why, alone among the animals, did you not attend my wedding feast?'

The tortoise replied:

'There's no place like home.'

This aroused the anger of Zeus and he condemned her to carry her home everywhere on her back.

It is thus that many prefer to live simply at home than to eat richly at the tables of others.

NOTE: The tortoise actually replied with 'Home is dear, home is best,' apparently a maxim of the Greeks, so we have used an equivalent maxim.

126

Zeus the Judge

Once upon a time, Zeus decided that Hermes should inscribe on ostraka the faults of men and deposit these ostraka in a little wooden box [*kibōtion*] near him, so that he could do justice in each case. But the ostraka got mixed up together and some came sooner, others later, to the hands of Zeus for him to pass judgements on them as they deserved.

This fable shows that one should not be surprised if wrong-doers and wicked people are not punished sooner after they commit their misdeeds.

NOTE: Ostraka were potsherds, bits of broken pots, or tablets made of earthernware, or even oyster shells, by which the ancient Greeks cast their votes in assemblies and on which they also made notes. A pile of ostraka was thus the ancient equivalent of a notepad.

As for the little wooden box, such boxes in mythological settings often indicate some special meaning. A chest, especially when it is called a *larnax* or a *soros*, may indicate that, as Professor H. J. Rose suspected, 'some kind of ritual lies behind all these tales'. See N. M. Holley, 'The Floating Chest', *Journal of Hellenic Studies* (Vol. LXIX, 1949, pp. 39–47). And see also Robert K. G. Temple, *He Who Saw Everything: A Verse Translation of the Epic of Gilgamesh* (Rider, 1991, pp. xxiii, 132, 134).

127

The Sun and the Frogs

It was summer, and people were celebrating the wedding feast of the Sun. All the animals were rejoicing at the event, and only the frogs were left to join in the gaiety. But a protesting frog called out:

'Fools! How can you rejoice? The Sun dries out all the marshland. If he takes a wife and has a child similar to himself, imagine how much more we would suffer!'

Plenty of empty-headed people are jubilant about things which they have no cause to celebrate.

128

The Mule

A mule who had grown fat on barley began to get frisky, saying to herself: 'My father is a fast-running horse, and I take after him in every way.' But, one day, she was forced to run a race. At the end of the race she looked glum and remembered that her father was really an ass.

This fable shows that even if circumstances put a man on show, he ought never to forget his origins, for life is full of uncertainty.

129

Herakles and Athena

Herakles was making his way through a narrow pass when he spotted something on the ground which looked like an apple. He decided to crush it, but the object doubled its size. When he saw this, Herakles stamped on it more violently than before and struck it with his club. The object swelled in volume and became so big that it blocked the road. The hero Herakles then dropped his club and stood there in a state of amazement. As this was going on, Athena appeared before him and said:

'Stop, brother. This thing is the spirit of dispute and quarrels. If one leaves it alone, it stays just as it was before. But if you fight it, see how it blows up.'

This fable shows that combat and strife are the cause of untold harm.

130

Herakles and Pluto

Herakles was admitted to the ranks of the gods and received at the table of Zeus, bowing graciously to each god in turn. Lastly he came to Pluto, God of Wealth. But he lowered his eyes to the floor and turned away from him. Shocked, Zeus asked why, having pleasantly saluted all the gods, he should turn his face away when he got to Pluto. Herakles replied:

'It's because when we were together on earth I nearly always saw him being attracted to wicked men.'

This fable could also apply to men who are made wealthy by fortune but who are of bad character.

131

The Demi-god [Hērōs]

A man had the image of a demi-god in his house and offered it rich sacrifices. As he didn't cease spending and using considerable sums for the sacrifices, the demi-god appeared before him one night and said:

'Stop squandering your wealth, my friend. For if you spend everything and become poor, you'll only take it out on me.'

Thus, many people, fallen on hard times because of their own folly, lay the blame on their gods.

132

The Tunny-fish and the Dolphin

A tunny-fish was pursued by a dolphin and splashed through the water with a great to-do. It was when the dolphin had almost caught him that the force of the tunny-fish's leap landed him on a sand bar. Carried by the same impulse, the dolphin landed beside him and there they both lay. As the tunny-fish took his last gasps and faced death he said:

'I no longer dread death now that I see he who has caused it sharing the same fate.'

This fable shows that it is easier to tolerate our misfortune when it is shared by those who have caused it.

NOTE: The fact that dolphins breathe air was clearly not realized here.

133

The Quack Doctor

A quack doctor once treated a sick man. All the other doctors he had consulted had told him that his life was not in any danger but that his recovery would be slow. Only the quack doctor advised him to settle all his affairs because he would not survive much more than a day, and then he left him to it.

A few days later the sick man got up and ventured outside. He was pale and walked with difficulty. He chanced to meet the quack doctor, who said to him:

'How are the inhabitants of the Underworld getting on?'

The sick man replied:

'They are at peace because they have drunk the Waters of Lēthē [Forgetfulness]. But recently there has been a great fuss down there. Both Death and Hades have issued terrible threats against all doctors, claiming that they won't allow the sick to die naturally. And they have written all their names down on a register. They were going to add your name to the list, but I threw myself at their feet and implored them not to, swearing that you are not a real doctor and had been unjustly accused of being one for no reason.'

This particular fable pillories those doctors whose science and talent consists solely of plausible words.

134

The Doctor and the Sick Man

A doctor had been looking after a patient, but the man died. And the doctor said to his household:

'This man would not be dead if he had abstained from wine and had taken his enemas.'

'Ha! My dear friend,' said one of his servants, 'it's no good saying that now when it's useless; it was when he was still alive and could benefit that you should have given him that advice.'

This fable shows that our friends should come to our aid at times of need and not make clever remarks when things are desperate.

135

The Kite and the Snake

A kite swooped down and carried off a snake but the snake twisted round and bit the bird. So the two of them then hurtled down from a great height and the kite was killed by the fall.

The snake declaimed:

'Why were you so stupid as to harm me, who had done nothing against you? It serves you right to be punished for having carried me off.'

People who give in to jealousy and hurt those who are weaker than themselves could fall into the same trap: they pay the price when all the harm they have done is unexpectedly revealed.

NOTE: Another version of this fable is found in Fable 167, 'The Raven and the Snake'.

136

The Kite Who Neighed

The kite once had a different voice, a voice which was high-pitched and shrill. But one day he heard a horse neighing beautifully, and he longed to imitate it. Try as he might, he simply couldn't attain the same voice as the horse, and at the same time he lost his own.

This is why he has neither his own voice nor that of the horse.

Jealous people envy qualities which they don't possess and lose their own.

137

The Bird-catcher and the Asp

A bird-catcher took his snare and birdlime and went out to do some hunting. He spotted a thrush on a tall tree and decided to try and catch it. So, having arranged his [sticky] twigs one on top of the other, he concentrated his attention upwards. While he was gazing thus he didn't see that he had trodden on a sleeping asp, which turned on him and bit him. The fowler, knowing that he was mortally wounded, said to himself:

'How unfortunate I am! I wanted to catch my prey and I did not see that I myself would become Death's prey.'

This is how, when we plot against our fellow-creatures, we are the first to fall into calamity.

NOTE: The asp, or Egyptian cobra [*Vipera aspis*], does not exist in Greece. This fable thus has its origins elsewhere.

The Greeks made birdlime, *ixos*, a sticky glue spread on the branches to which the birds' feet got stuck, usually from crushed mistletoe berries, though sometimes from oak-gum or other sticky substances. See also Fables 157, 242 and 349.

138

The Old Horse

An old horse had been sold to a miller to turn the millstone. When he was harnessed to the mill-wheel he groaned and exclaimed:

'From the turn of the race course I am reduced to such a turn as this!'

Don't be too proud of youthful strength, for many a man's old age is spent in hard work.

139

The Horse, the Ox, the Dog
and the Man

When Zeus made man, he only gave him a short life-span. But man, making use of his intelligence, made a house and lived in it when winter came on. Then, one day, it became fiercely cold, it poured with rain and the horse could no longer endure it. So he galloped up to the man's house and asked if he could take shelter with him. But the man said that he could only shelter there on one condition, and that was that the horse would give him a portion of the years of his life. The horse gave him some willingly.

A short time later, the ox also appeared. He too could not bear the bad weather any more. The man said the same thing to him, that he wouldn't give him shelter unless the ox gave him a certain number of his own years. The ox gave him some and was allowed to go in.

Finally the dog, dying of cold, also appeared, and upon surrendering part of the time he had left to live, was given shelter.

Thus it resulted that for that portion of time originally allotted them by Zeus, men are pure and good; when they reach the years gained from the horse, they are glorious and proud; when they reach the years of the ox, they are willing to accept discipline; but when they reach the dog years, they become grumbling and irritable.

One could apply this fable to surly old men.

140

The Horse and the Groom

A groom used to steal his horse's barley and sell it. To make up for it he spent the whole day grooming and currying the horse, who said to him:

'If you really want to see me look good, don't sell the barley that is intended to feed me.'

Thus, greedy people trick poor people with their seductive talk and with flattery, while depriving them of their bare necessities.

141

The Horse and the Ass

A man had a horse and an ass. One day, while they were on the road, the ass said to the horse:

'Take a bit of my burden if you value my life.'

The horse turned a deaf ear and the ass fell, exhausted, and died.

Then the master transferred the load on to the horse, as well as the flayed skin of the ass. The horse sighed and said:

'Ah! I don't stand a chance! Alas, what has befallen me! Because I didn't want to carry a light load, now here I am carrying it all, even the skin as well!'

This fable shows that if the strong stand by the weak, they preserve each other's lives.

142

The Horse and the Soldier

A soldier fed his horse well on barley as long as it was his companion, sharing all his toils and dangers for the duration of the war. But when the war ended the horse was used to do menial work and to carry heavy loads, and was only given straw to eat. Meanwhile, another war was declared and, at the sound of the trumpet, the master bridled his horse, armed himself and mounted. But the horse, having no strength, stumbled at each step. He said to his master:

'Now go and line up among the foot-soldiers. For from a horse you have changed me into an ass. How do you expect me to change back from an ass into a horse again?'

In times of security and ease, misfortunes should not be forgotten.

143

The Reed and the Olive

The reed and the olive tree were arguing over their steadfastness, strength and ease. The olive taunted the reed for his powerlessness and pliancy in the face of all the winds. The reed kept quiet and didn't say a word. Then, not long after this, the wind blew violently. The reed, shaken and bent, escaped easily from it, but the olive tree, resisting the wind, was snapped by its force.

The story shows that people who yield to circumstances and to superior power have the advantage over their stronger rivals.

144

The Camel Who Shat in the River

A camel was crossing a swiftly flowing river. He shat and immediately saw his own dung floating in front of him, carried by the rapidity of the current.

'What is that there?' he asked himself. 'That which was behind me I now see pass in front of me.'

This applies to a situation where the rabble and the idiots hold sway rather than the eminent and the sensible.

NOTE: Once again, this fable cannot be of Greek origin, since Greek camels, if they existed, would never do anything so improper.

145

The Camel, the Elephant
and the Ape

The animals were consulting together on the choice of a king. The camel and the elephant admired themselves in the ranks of animals and argued over their vote, hoping to be chosen from among the others thanks to their great stature and their strength. But the ape declared that neither of them was suitable to reign: 'The camel,' he said, 'because he never shows anger against wrongdoers, and the elephant because he runs away from piglets – a creature of which he is terrified – so he could never defend his subjects from them.'

This fable shows that sometimes it is only a small thing that bars the path to a great position.

NOTE: As so often happens in the fables, this one concerns animals, none of which, except pigs, existed in Greece.

146

The Camel and Zeus

The camel, seeing the bull have the advantage of horns, was envious of him and wanted to acquire some too. He went to find Zeus and begged him to furnish him with some horns. But Zeus, angry that he was not content already with his great size and with his strength, and wanted yet more, not only refused to add some horns but proceeded to cut off a portion of his ears.

So it is that many people, through greed, look upon others with envy, not realizing that they are losing their own advantages.

147

The Dancing Camel

A camel, who was forced to dance by his master, said:
   'It is not only when I dance that I lack grace; I even lack it when I walk.'

This fable could apply to all acts bereft of grace.

148

The Camel Seen for the First Time

When they first set eyes on a camel, men were afraid. Awed by its huge size, they ran away. But when, in time, they realized its gentleness, they plucked up enough courage to approach it. Then, gradually realizing that it had no temper, they went up to it and grew to hold it in such contempt that they put a bridle on it and gave it to the children to lead.

This fable shows that habit can overcome the fear which awesome things inspire.

149

The Two Scarab Beetles

A bull grazed on a little island and two scarab beetles nourished themselves on his dung. As winter approached, one of them said to the other that he thought he would cross over to the mainland. He said he would chance it and go and spend the winter across the strait. If he found plenty of food there he would bring him some. He pointed out that there would be more for the other beetle to eat if he were alone.

So the beetle flew across the water to the mainland where he came across many fresh dung droppings. He settled himself down on them and began to eat heartily. The winter passed and he flew back to the island. His friend, seeing him so fat and healthy, reminded him of his promise and reproached him for never coming back for him. But the selfish beetle replied:

'Oh, don't blame me. It's simply the nature of the locality, you know. True, you can find enough to live on there, but you just can't bring it back with you.'

One could apply this fable to those who are superficial friends, entertaining in company but hopeless at being any help otherwise.

150

The Crab and the Fox

A crab, having climbed up out of the sea on to the shore, was pursuing his solitary life. A starving fox spotted him and, as he had not a scrap of food to put between his teeth, he ran up and pounced on the crab to devour him. As he was about to be eaten, the crab cried out:

'I deserve this fate! I, who lived in the sea, had the folly to imagine I could live on the land!'

It is thus with men also: those who abandon their own occupations to mix themselves up in affairs which don't concern them meet with misfortune as a natural consequence.

151

The Crab and Her Mother

'Don't walk sideways,' said a mother crab to her child, 'and don't drag your sides against the wet rock.'

'Mother,' the young crab replied, 'if you want to teach me, walk straight yourself. I will watch you and then I will copy you.'

When one reproves others, it is just as well to live straight and walk straight oneself before starting to preach a lesson.

152

The Walnut Tree

A walnut tree which grew on the edge of a path was constantly hit by a volley of stones. It said to itself with a sigh:

'How unlucky I am that year after year I attract insults and suffering.'

This fable is aimed at people who don't withdraw from a source of annoyance for their own good.

153

The Beaver

The beaver is a four-footed animal who lives in pools. A beaver's genitals serve, it is said, to cure certain ailments. So when the beaver is spotted and pursued to be mutilated – since he knows why he is being hunted – he will run for a certain distance, and he will use the speed of his feet to remain intact. But when he sees himself about to be caught, he will bite off his own parts, throw them, and thus save his own life.

Among men also, those are wise who, if attacked for their money, will sacrifice it rather than lose their lives.

NOTE: It was believed in antiquity that the valued secretion *castorea* was obtained from the beaver's scrotum, hence 'biting off his own parts' in the fable. We now know that the secretion is found in two separate sacs and not actually in the scrotum. The name of the beaver in Greek is *castōr*, the same as the twin-god, and also the same as one name given to the crocus, source of saffron. There is little doubt that a complex of mythological meanings is involved here. A cognate word is found in Sanskrit, *kasturi(kā)* or *kastūri(kā)*, meaning both 'musk deer' and 'musk', and thus referring to the secretions of the musk deer rather than the beaver. Since these word forms are isolated in both Greek and Sanskrit, they are probably loan-words originating from a very early trade in aromatic animal secretions supplied by Indo-European tribes to the Middle East.

The etymology of the words is probably from the Egyptian *qas*, or *qes*. That word means 'efflux' and, because it also means 'vomit', the Egyptians probably applied the same word to ambergris, which is whale vomit, and the substances castorea and musk. The word also means 'to prepare a mummy for burial', so we suspect that the uses of these substances were for mummification. The same Egyptian word means 'fetters that bind' (i.e. also mummy-wrappings), and the Greek god Castor was reputed to be the inventor of manacles, thus probably carrying over an Egyptian pun at an early date. An apparent cognate with the Egyptian is found in Akkadian, where *kasitu* means 'being bound or fettered', from *kasu*, 'to bind'. Curiously, the Akkadian *kāsistu*, with the long initial vowel, refers to a rodent, from *kasāsu*, 'to gnaw' or 'gnaw through', which is, of course, so characteristic of the beaver.

Aristotle, our chief Greek zoological authority, was uneasy about the word *castōr* as applied to the beaver. He actually speaks of the 'so-called *castōr*' (*kaloumenos castōr*) in the *History of Animals* (594b31), and proceeds to call the beaver by the name which he clearly regarded as its true name, *latax* (487a22 and 594b32), and which he describes as cutting down the riverside aspens or poplars with its teeth. Aristotle seems to have suspected that *castōr* was a synonym for the beaver arising from some unusual source, which we can see was probably by association from the name for its aromatic secretion being applied to the animal itself.

154

The Gardener Watering the Vegetables

A man passed a gardener who was watering his vegetables and he stopped to ask him why the wild vegetables were flourishing and vigorous while the cultivated ones were sickly and puny.

The gardener replied: 'It's because the Earth is a mother to the one and a stepmother to the others.'

Similarly, the children fed by a stepmother are not nourished like those who have their true mother.

155

The Gardener and the Dog

The gardener's dog had fallen down a well. Wanting to save it, the gardener went down the well himself. But the dog, imagining that the gardener was going to push him down even further, turned around and bit him. The gardener, in pain from this wound, climbed out, saying:

'It's all the same to me. Why should I put myself out to save the beast when he wants to perish?'

This fable is addressed to those who are ungrateful and unjust.

156

The Kithara-player

A kithara-player, devoid of talent, sang from morning to night in a house with thickly plastered walls. As the walls echoed with his own sounds he imagined that he had a very beautiful voice. He so overestimated his own voice from then on that he decided to perform in a theatre. But he sang so badly on the stage that he was driven off it by people throwing stones.

Thus, certain orators who, at school, seem to have some talent, reveal their incompetence as soon as they enter the political arena.

157

The Thrush

A thrush was pecking berries in a myrtle grove and, infatuated by their sweetness, was unable to leave it. A fowler observed her satisfying herself there and caught her in a lime-trap. Then, as she was about to be killed, the thrush said:

'Wretch that I am! For the pleasure of eating I deprive myself of life!'

This fable is directed at the debauched who are lost in pleasure.

158

The Thieves and the Cock

Some thieves who broke into a house found nothing there but a cockerel. They took it and went away. As he was about to be sacrificed by them, the cock begged them to release him, pleading that he was useful to men in rousing them by night for their work.

'All the more reason to kill you,' they said, 'for by waking men up you prevent us from thieving.'

This fable shows that the more you thwart the bad, you render service to the good.

NOTE: The cockerel boasts of crowing *nyktōr*, an adverb meaning 'by night'. He does not refer to dawn. This must mean that Greeks often rose well before daybreak.

159

The Stomach and the Feet

The stomach and the feet were arguing over their strength. The feet constantly alleged that they were much superior in strength because they carried the stomach. To this the stomach replied:

'But, my friends, if I don't provide you with nourishment, you won't be able to carry me.'

Thus it is with armies: generally speaking, numbers count for nothing if the commanders are not sensible.

160

The Jackdaw and the Fox

There was once a jackdaw suffering from hunger who sat for ages on the branch of a fig tree. He had seen that the figs were still green, so he decided to wait for them to ripen. A fox saw him sitting there endlessly and asked him the reason. Upon hearing why, the fox said:

'You've got it all wrong, friend. You're just living off hope. Hope feeds illusions but not the stomach.'

This fable applies to the covetous.

161

The Jackdaw and the Ravens

A jackdaw who grew larger in size than the other jackdaws disdained their company. So he took himself off to the ravens and asked if he could share his life with them. But the ravens, unfamiliar with his shape and his voice, mobbed him and chased him away. So, rejected by them, he went back to be with the jackdaws. But the jackdaws, outraged at his defection, refused to have him back. And thus he was an outcast from the society of both jackdaws and ravens.

It is similar with people. Those who abandon their own country in preference for another are in low esteem there for being foreigners, but despised by their compatriots because they have scorned them.

162

The Jackdaw and the Birds

Wishing to establish a King of the Birds, Zeus set a date for summoning them all before him for comparison: he would choose the most beautiful one to reign over them. The birds went off then to the shallow water near the shore of a river to wash. Now the jackdaw, realizing his ugliness, went around gathering up the feathers which fell from the other birds, which he then arranged and attached to his own body. Thus he became the most handsome of all.

Then the big day arrived and all the birds presented themselves before Zeus. The jackdaw, with his motley adornment, was among them. And Zeus voted for him to be the royal bird on account of his beauty. But the other birds, outraged at this decision, each pulled out the feather that had come from him. The result was that the jackdaw was stripped and once again became just a jackdaw.

Likewise with men who have debts: as long as they possess the wealth of other people, they seem to be somebody. But when they have paid their debts they find that they are once again their old selves.

NOTE: This fable was doubtless suggested by the jackdaw's actual habit of collecting colourful bits, including other birds' feathers, for its nest.

163

The Jackdaw and the Pigeons

A jackdaw, espying some well-fed pigeons in a pigeon-rearing aviary, whitened his plumage and joined them to share some of their food. So long as he stayed silent, the pigeons took him to be one of their own kind and approved of him as he mingled among them. But then, for a moment, he forgot himself and let out a cry. Upon hearing his unfamiliar voice the pigeons chased him away. So, having become familiar with how sumptuously the pigeons fared, he now had to return to the jackdaws. But the jackdaws didn't recognize him any more because of his colour and they rejected him and wouldn't allow him into their company either. So, having wanted the food of both, he now had neither.

This fable shows that we ought to be content with our lot. It also tells us that not only does covetousness serve for nothing, but it often causes us to lose that which we already possess.

NOTE: See Aristotle, *History of Animals* (593a16). *Peristeras*, the word for the common pigeon, is there distinguished from four other related ornithological terms, such as woodpigeon.

164

The Jackdaw Who Escaped

A man trapped a jackdaw and, attaching a flaxen thread to its foot, gave it to his child. But the jackdaw could not resign himself to living in captivity. He took advantage of an unguarded moment and flew off back to his nest. But the thread got caught up in the branches and the bird couldn't fly away. On the point of death, he said:

'How wretched is my lot! For, not being able to bear slavery to man, I was unaware that I was depriving myself of my life.'

This fable could be addressed to men who, in wishing to defend themselves against moderate dangers, may be throwing themselves unawares into more deadly peril.

165

The Raven and the Fox

A raven stole a piece of meat and flew up and perched on a branch with it. A fox saw him there and determined to get the meat for himself. So he sat at the base of the tree and said to the raven:

'Of all the birds you are by far the most beautiful. You have such elegant proportions, are so stately and sleek. You were ideally made to be the king of all the birds. And if you only had a voice you would surely be the king.'

The raven, wanting to demonstrate to him that there was nothing wrong with his voice, dropped the meat and uttered a great cry. The fox rushed forward, pounced on the meat, and said:

'Oh, raven, if only you also had judgement, you would want for nothing to be the king of the birds.'

This fable is a lesson to all fools.

NOTE: Two versions of this fable occur in India. Both are preserved in the Buddhist collection of 'Jātaka Tales', many of which are pre-Buddhist. One version is number 294. In this version, a jackal persuades a crow to shake the branch of a fruit tree so that he can get some fruit. In the other version, number 295, the crow sees a jackal eating a carcass and devises flattery to try and get some meat from the jackal. Another Jātaka tale, number 215, describes a tortoise being carried through the air while he bites on a stick and by opening his mouth to speak, he falls and is killed; this motif is somewhat similar to the Aesop fable of being undone by opening one's mouth and letting go of something.

166

The Raven and Hermes

A raven who was caught in a snare promised the god Apollo that if he could get free he would offer some frankincense to him. But when his wish was granted he forgot his vow.

Later, caught in another snare, the raven abandoned Apollo to address his plea to the god Hermes, to whom he promised a sacrifice. But Hermes replied to him:

'Oh, wretched raven, how can I trust you, who have disavowed your first master and cheated him?'

When one shows ingratitude towards a benefactor, one can no longer count on help from others in times of need.

167

The Raven and the Snake

A raven who was short of food espied a snake sleeping in the sun; he swooped down, seized it and flew away with it. But the snake twisted round and bit him, and the raven said as he was about to die:

'How unlucky I was to find a windfall of such a kind that it would murder me!'

One could say that this fable applies to the man who discovers a treasure that threatens his life.

NOTE: This fable is another version of Fable 135, 'The Kite and the Snake'.

168

The Sick Raven

A sick raven said to its mother:

'Pray to the gods, Mother, and don't weep.'

The mother said:

'My child, which of the gods would take pity on you? Is there one among them from whom you have not stolen food?'

This fable shows that those who make many enemies in life will not find friends in their hour of need.

NOTE: The theft of food refers to ravens stealing pieces of the offerings left on altars and in temples, or even taking bits during actual sacrificial ceremonies.

169

The Crested Lark

A crested lark, caught in a snare, lamented:

'Alas! What an unlucky bird I am! I have not stolen anything from anyone, neither money nor gold nor anything precious. It is only a little grain of wheat that has caused my death.'

This fable applies to those people who, for the sake of a paltry profit, expose themselves to a great danger.

NOTE: We have evidence from Aristophanes in *The Birds* (471) that there was another Aesop fable about the crested lark, which is lost. In that strange mythological fable, the crested lark was said to have been created before anything else, and when her father died she could find no burial place because the Earth did not yet exist, so 'on the fifth day' she buried him in her head – i.e. her crest – as there was nowhere else available. Unfortunately, this bizarre tale is known only from the cursory remarks of Aristophanes and has not otherwise been preserved, so that we cannot make proper sense of it.

170

The Chough and the Raven

The chough became envious of the raven because he gave presages and omens to men, being a bird of augury who foretold things to come. He resolved to attain the same status. So, seeing some travellers pass by, he went and perched on a nearby tree and let out great cries. Hearing this, the travellers turned round, startled. But one of them spoke up:

'Come on, friends. Let's continue our journey. It's only a chough. His cries are not an omen.'

It is also like this with men: those who compete with rivals stronger than themselves will not only be unequal to them, but they will also become a laughing stock.

171

The Chough and the Dog

A chough offered up a sacrifice to Athena and invited a dog to the sacrificial banquet. The dog said to him:

'Why are you so lavish with these useless sacrifices? The goddess actually detests you and is on the point of discrediting your omens and portents.'

To which the chough replied:

'But it is precisely because of this that I offer sacrifice to her: I know she is badly disposed to me in this way and I want to be reconciled with her.'

Likewise, many people don't hesitate to help their enemies because they are afraid of them.

172

The Snails

A ploughman's child was baking some snails. Hearing them sputtering, he said:

'Stupid creatures! Your houses are on fire yet you sing!'

This fable shows that everything one does inopportunely is reprehensible.

173

The Swan Mistaken for a Goose

A wealthy man kept a goose and a swan together, not for the same purpose, but the one for his voice and the other destined for the table. When the time came for the goose to meet his fate it was night and it became impossible to distinguish between the two birds. But the swan, who had been caught by mistake instead of the goose, began to sing as a prelude to his own demise. His voice was recognized and the song saved his life.

This fable demonstrates how music can cause death to be delayed.

NOTE: The premise of this fable is the odd tradition of 'the swan song' – the ancient belief that a swan about to die ended its life with a baleful song. At some point in the unknown past, some such strange incident must have happened and the story was repeated until it became a legend. See also the next fable, Fable 174. Which is stranger – that this story came to be believed by everyone in ancient Greece or that we still use the expression 'swan song' today?

174

The Swan and His Owner

It is said that swans sing when they are about to die. Now, a man came across a swan for sale and, knowing by hearsay that this was a very melodious creature, he bought it. One day, when he was giving a dinner, he went and fetched the swan and urged it to sing during the feast. The swan remained silent. But soon after, sensing that he was going to die, he sang a dirge to himself. His master, upon hearing this, said to him:

'If you will only sing when you are about to die, I was a fool to request you to sing before; I should have prepared to sacrifice you and then you would have sung!'

Thus it happens sometimes that what we don't wish to do out of good grace we do under compulsion.

175

The Two Dogs

A man owned two dogs. The first he trained to hunt and the second he ordered to guard the house. Now when the one went hunting and caught some game, the master threw a piece of it to the other dog as well. The hunting dog was aggrieved at this and reproached his friend, saying that it was he who had gone out and had a hard time of it on every occasion, while his comrade did nothing yet enjoyed the fruits of his labour. The guard dog replied:

'Ah! You should not blame me but our master, for it was he who taught me not to work and to live instead from the work of others.'

Thus, lazy children are not to blame when their parents have brought them up to be idle.

176

The Starving Dogs

Some starving dogs saw some hides soaking in a river. Unable to reach them, they agreed that between them they would drink up all the water to reach the skins. But it happened that before they reached the skins the dogs burst from the force of the water they had drunk.

Thus some men, in the hope of a profit, submit to dangerous work but lose it before having obtained the object of their desires.

177

The Man Bitten by a Dog

A man who had been bitten by a dog roamed far and wide, looking for someone to heal his wound. Someone told him all he had to do was wipe the blood from his wound with some bread and throw the bread to the dog which had bitten him. To this the injured man replied:

'But if I did that, every dog in the city would bite me.'

Similarly, if you indulge someone's wickedness, you provoke him to do even more harm.

178

The Dog Entertained as a Guest
(or *The Man and His Dog*)

A man prepared a dinner to entertain a family friend. His dog invited another dog.

'Friend,' the dog said, 'come to the house to dine with me.'

His guest arrived full of joy and stopped to have a look at all the food laid out, muttering to himself:

'Oh! What a godsend for me! I am going to guzzle and give myself such a bellyful that I won't be hungry all day tomorrow!'

All the while he said this his tail wagged as he showed his trust in his friend.

The cook, seeing his tail go to and fro, seized him by the paws and hurled him out of the window. The dog went home howling. Along the way he met some other dogs. One of them asked him:

'How was your dinner?'

The dog replied:

'I had so many drinks I became completely drunk. I don't even know how I got out of the house.'

This fable shows that you shouldn't trust those who are generous with other people's fare.

179

The Hunting Hound
and the Dogs

A dog reared in a house was trained to fight wild beasts. One day, when he saw several of them lined up in battle array, he broke loose from the dog collar round his throat and ran off through the streets. Other dogs, seeing him as bulky as a bull, said to him:

'Why are you running away?'

'I know well,' he replied, 'that I live amid plenty and have more than enough to eat, but I am always close to death, fighting as I do with bears and lions.'

Then the other dogs said to each other:

'Although poor, we have a good life for we don't have to fight with lions or bears.'

It is not necessary to court danger for sumptuous living or vainglory but, on the contrary, to shun it.

NOTE: Dogs were often trained to fight wild beasts to provide entertainment for people living in towns.

180

The Dog, the Cock
and the Fox

A dog and a cockerel, having made friends, were strolling along a road together. As evening fell, the cockerel flew up into a tree to sleep there, and the dog went to sleep at the foot of the tree, which was hollow.

According to his habit, the cockerel crowed just before daybreak. This alerted a fox nearby, who ran up to the tree and called up to the cockerel:

'Do come down, sir, for I dearly wish to embrace a creature who could have such a beautiful voice as you!'

The cockerel said:

'I shall come down as soon as you awaken the doorkeeper who is asleep at the foot of the tree.'

Then, as the fox went to look for the 'doorkeeper', the dog pounced briskly on him and tore him to pieces.

This fable teaches us that sensible men, when their enemies attack them, divert them to someone better able to defend them than they are themselves.

181

The Dog and the Shellfish

There was a dog who used to swallow eggs. One day he saw a shellfish. He opened his mouth and snapped his jaws shut again violently, swallowing it, because he thought it was an egg. But, feeling a heaviness in his bowels, he became ill and said:

'I only got what I deserve – I, who assume that everything round is an egg.'

This fable teaches us that those who undertake things recklessly get themselves into strange predicaments.

182

The Dog and the Hare

A hunting hound seized a hare and attempted both to bite it and lick its chops at the same time. The hare tired of this and said:

'Hey you, either bite me or kiss me, so that I can know whether you are enemy or friend.'

This fable applies to an ambiguous man.

183

The Dog and the Butcher

A dog bounded into a butcher's shop and seized a heart while the butcher was busy, and then made his getaway. Turning round, the butcher saw him flee with it and shouted:

· 'Hey, you! Wherever you may run to, I'll have my eye on you. For you haven't made me lose heart but caused me to take heart.'

This fable shows that accidents are often an education for men.

NOTE: The Greek *double entendre* can fortunately be preserved in English, which has the same idiomatic usages for the word 'heart'.

184

The Sleeping Dog and
the Wolf

A dog lay asleep in front of a farm building. A wolf pounced on him and was going to make a meal of him, when the dog begged him not to eat him straight away:

'At the moment,' he said, 'I am thin and lean. But wait a little while; my masters will be celebrating a wedding feast. I will get some good mouthfuls and will fatten up and will be a much better meal for you.'

The wolf believed him and went on his way. A little while later he came back and found the dog asleep on top of the house. He stopped below and shouted up to him, reminding him of their agreement. Then the dog said:

'Oh, wolf! If you ever see me asleep in front of the farm again, don't wait for the wedding banquet!'

This fable shows that wise people, when they get out of a fix, take care of themselves all the rest of their life.

185

The Dog Who Carried the Meat

A dog was crossing a river holding a piece of meat in his mouth. Catching sight of his reflection in the water, he believed that it was another dog who was holding a bigger piece of meat. So, dropping his own piece, he leaped into the water to take the piece from the other dog. But the result was that he ended up with neither piece – one didn't even exist and the other was swept away by the current.

This fable applies to the covetous.

186

The Dog with a Bell

A dog furtively bit people, so his master hung a bell on him to warn everyone he was coming. Then the dog, shaking his bell, swaggered about in the agora. An old bitch said to him:

'What have you got to strut about? You don't wear the bell as a result of any virtue, but to advertise your secret ill nature.'

The secret spitefulness of boastful people is exposed by their vainglorious behaviour.

187

The Dog Who Chased a Lion, and the Fox

A hunting hound, having spotted a lion, set off in pursuit of him. But the lion turned on him and began to roar. Then the dog took fright and turned back.

A fox saw this and said to the dog:

'My poor fellow, you chased a lion but you couldn't even endure his roar!'

One could relate this fable with regard to presumptuous people who mix with those more powerful than themselves in order to denigrate them, but then turn and run away when faced by them.

188

The Gnat and the Lion

A gnat once approached a lion and said:

'I'm not afraid of you because you're not any stronger than me! And if you think otherwise, show me what you can do! You can scratch with your claws and bite with your teeth. But that's no more than a woman can do to her husband. As for myself, I am more powerful than you, and if you don't think so, let's fight!'

Sounding his horn, the gnat swooped down on the lion, flew into his nostrils, biting him there and on the hairless parts of his face. The lion tore himself with his own claws until, unable to get hold of the gnat, he was forced to give up. The gnat, having vanquished the lion, buzzed around sounding his horn, chanted a victory song and flew off.

But, shortly afterwards, the gnat became entangled in a spider's web and was eaten. As he was being devoured, he wailed:

'I, who defeated the strongest of all creatures, am destroyed by a mere spider!'

189

The Gnat and the Bull

A gnat had settled on a bull's horn. After he had been there for a while and was about to fly off, he asked the bull whether he would, after all, like him to go away. The bull replied:

'When you came, I didn't feel you. And when you go I won't feel you either.'

One could apply this fable to the feeble person whose presence or absence is neither helpful nor harmful.

NOTE: This same fable, but with an elephant instead of a bull, occurs in ancient Sumer and is at least 2,000 years earlier than classical Greece. The compiler of the Aesop collection may have changed the elephant to a bull because otherwise the point of Fable 210, which features an elephant terrified of a gnat instead of indifferent to it, would have been wholly lost.

190

The Hares and the Foxes

One day, the hares, being at war with the eagles, called the foxes to come to their aid.

'We would come to help you,' called the foxes, 'if we didn't know who you are and with whom you are fighting!'

This fable shows that those who come into conflict with persons who are more powerful despise safety.

191

The Hares and the Frogs

One day, the hares had a gathering to moan among themselves about having such a precarious and fearful existence. Were they not, in effect, the prey of men, of dogs, of eagles and of other animals as well? Would it not be better to perish once and for all than to live in terror?

This resolution was taken, and they all dashed at once towards the pond in order to throw themselves in and drown there. But the frogs, who were squatting around the pond, had no sooner heard the noise of the hares running towards them than they leaped into the water. At this, one of the hares who was in the lead, said:

'Stop, comrades! Do not do yourselves harm! For come and see – there are some animals here who are even more fearful than we are!'

This fable shows that the unfortunate console themselves by seeing people who are worse off than themselves.

192

The Hare and the Fox

The hare, wishing to ingratiate himself with the fox to avoid trouble, said:

'I know you are called wily. But I have heard it is really because you know how to while away the hours better than anybody else. Is that so?'

'If you have any doubts,' replied the fox, 'come to my place and I will entertain you to dinner and show you how I pass an evening.'

The hare followed him home. Once inside, the fox had nothing for dinner but the hare. As it realized its fate, the hare bewailed:

'Oh, to learn by such misfortune! For I see that your name truly comes from your wiles.'

Great misfortunes often happen to the curious who abandon themselves to a clumsy indiscretion.

NOTE: The Greek original is based upon a non-translatable pun using the word *kerdos*, which means both 'profit' and 'wily'. We have substituted an English pun which, although the meaning is not exact, gives some impression of the fable. In the original the hare ingratiatingly says he thinks the fox is really called *wily* only because he knows how to make a *profit*, but discovers how wrong he is!

193

The Seagull and the Kite

A gull ruptured his gullet swallowing a fish and lay dead on the beach. A kite spotted him and said:

'You only got what you deserved, since, being born a bird, you looked for your living in the sea.'

Thus, those who abandon their real trade to take up one alien to them are deservedly unfortunate.

194

The Lioness and the Vixen

A vixen criticized a lioness for only ever bearing one child.

'Only one,' she said, 'but a lion.'

Do not judge merit by quantity, but by worth.

195

The Royalty of the Lion

A lion who became king didn't get angry and was neither cruel nor violent, but gentle and just, like a man might be.

During his reign, the Lion King called a general assembly of all the birds and beasts for the purpose of sanctioning legal arrangements to bind the wolf and the lamb to live together in perfect peace and harmony, as well as the panther and the chamois, the tiger and the deer, and the dog and the hare.

At the great assembly a hare was heard to say:

'How I have longed to see this day! The weak can take their place at the side of the strong without fear!'

When justice reigns in the state and all judgements are fair, the meek may also live in tranquillity.

196

The Ageing Lion
and the Fox

A lion who was getting old and could no longer obtain his food by force decided that he must resort to trickery instead. So he retired to a cave and lay down pretending to be ill. Thus, whenever any animals came to his cave to visit him, he ate them all as they appeared.

When many animals had disappeared, a fox figured out what was happening. He went to see the lion but stood at a safe distance outside the cave and asked him how he was.

'Oh, not very well,' said the lion. 'But why don't you come in?'

But the fox said:

'I would come inside if I hadn't seen that a lot of footprints are pointing inwards towards your cave but none are pointing out.'

Wise men note the indications of dangers and thus avoid them.

197

The Shut-in Lion and
the Ploughman

A lion entered a ploughman's animal shed. The ploughman, wishing to capture him, shut the door behind him. When he found that he was trapped, the lion killed all the sheep and ate them, and then attacked all the cattle. The ploughman became so alarmed for his own safety that he opened the door and the lion escaped as quickly as he could.

After the lion had disappeared, the ploughman's wife finding him wailing, came up to him and said:

'Well, it serves you right. How could you want to shut up the lion, a beast who ought to make you tremble even at a distance?'

People who incite the powerful must bear the consequences of their own folly.

198

The Amorous Lion and the Ploughman

A lion once fell in love with the daughter of a ploughman and asked for her hand in marriage. Not being able either to make up his mind to give his daughter to a ferocious beast or to refuse him because he feared him so much, the ploughman thought up the following idea. As the lion continued to press him, he told him that he deemed him worthy to be the husband of his daughter, but decided that he could give her to him on one condition, that he would pull out his teeth and cut his claws, for it was those that frightened the young girl.

The lion willingly resigned himself to this double sacrifice because he loved her. But, no sooner had he done this than the ploughman had nothing but contempt for him and, when he presented himself, drove him from his door with many blows.

This fable shows that those who too readily trust others, once deprived of their natural advantages, are easy prey to those who had previously feared them.

199

The Lion, the Fox
and the Stag

The lion had fallen ill and was resting in a cave. He said to the fox, who was his friend and with whom he did a bit of business from time to time:

'If you want me to live and be fierce again, go and beguile with honeyed words the big stag who lives in the forest, bring him to me so that I can get my paws on him. For I long to sink my teeth into his entrails and to eat his heart.'

The fox took himself off into the country and found the stag, who was leaping about in the forest. He approached the stag with a fond air, saluted him respectfully and said:

'I come to announce good news. You know that our king, the lion, is my neighbour. He is now very ill and on the point of death. He is demanding to know which animal will reign after him. The wild boar is lacking in all intelligence, the bear is awkward, the panther is irascible, the tiger is boastful. Only the stag is dignified enough to reign. For he is the tallest and longest-lived and, besides, his horn is deadly to snakes. But why go on any more? He has decided that you should become king. But now that I have brought you this good news, what may I have for being the bearer of it? Speak, for I am in the most terrible hurry, as I am afraid His Majesty will call me back. He cannot do without my counsel.

'If you would wish to listen to the words of an old fox, I would advise you to come with me and wait nearby for His Majesty's death.'

Thus spoke the fox. The stag's heart swelled with vanity at these words and he went to the cave without suspecting what would happen. Then the lion leaped at him headlong. However, he merely managed to tear the stag's ears with his claws. The stag saved himself and fled with all haste to the woods.

The fox clapped his hands in dismay at the loss of all his labour and the lion began to moan and make great roars, for he was overcome with hunger as well as with sorrow. He begged the fox to devise another way to beguile the stag.

The fox replied:

'It is an arduous and difficult task that you ask of me. Nevertheless, I will serve you once more.'

And then, like a hound he followed the scent of the stag towards the forest, plotting deceit as he ran. He stopped to ask some shepherds if they had seen a bleeding stag. They pointed towards his resting-place in the wood. The fox came upon the stag resting to get his second wind and presented himself shamelessly to him. The stag, full of anger and with his fur all splattered with blood, cursed him:

'You scoundrel, you will never get me to go to the lion's den again. If you so much as come near me once more you will pay with your life. Go and fox others who don't know you. Go and choose other beasts to make into kings and get them all excited about it!'

The fox replied:

'Are you so cowardly and faint-hearted? Is this distrust the reward that you give us, your good friends? The lion, in taking hold of your ear, was going to give you counsel and instruct you on the matter of your regal duties, in the manner of someone about to die. But you, you cannot even take a scratch from the paw of a sick lion! At the moment His Majesty is angrier than you are and wants to elevate the wolf to the kingship.'

And the fox continued:

'Alas! My poor wretched master! But come, do not be afraid. Be as meek as a lamb. For, I swear by all the leaves of the trees and by all the springs that you have absolutely no cause to fear the lion. As for me, my only wish is to serve you.'

In thus deceiving the unfortunate stag, the fox induced him once more to go to the cave of the lion. When the stag entered the lion's cave, the lion had him for supper. He swallowed all the bones, all the marrow and the entrails. The fox stood there watching him. The stag's heart fell to the ground. The fox snatched it and ate it to compensate himself for all his efforts. But the lion, having looked around for every morsel, could not find the heart, and asked where it was.

The fox, keeping his distance, said:

'The truth is, the stag had no heart. Don't even bother to look for it. For how could an animal be said to have a heart who has gone twice into a lion's den and encountered the paws of a lion?'

Thus, love of honour confuses Reason and closes the eyes to imminent danger.

200

The Lion, the Bear
and the Fox

A lion and a bear, having found the carcass of a faun, were battling over who should have it. They mauled each other so badly that they lost consciousness and lay half-dead. A fox, who happened to pass by and saw them lying there, unable to move, with the faun between them, ran into their midst, grabbed the carcass and escaped with it.

The lion and the bear, unable to get up because of the bad state they were in, murmured to each other:

'What fools we are! We've gone to all this trouble just for a fox!'

This fable shows that people have good reason to be annoyed when they see the results of their hard work carried off by chance.

201

The Lion and the Frog

A lion, hearing a frog croak, roared back, thinking that such a sound must come from some large creature. He waited for a while, then saw the creature emerge from a pond, went up to it and crushed it with his foot, saying:

'So much noise from one so small!'

This fable applies to people who are all noise and have no substance to them.

202

The Lion and the Dolphin

A lion was roaming along the seashore when he saw a dolphin raise its head up out of the waves. The lion proposed an alliance of friendship between them.

'You and I are most suited to be friends and allies,' he said. 'For I'm the king of all the beasts on the land and you are the ruler of all the creatures of the sea.'

The dolphin willingly agreed.

Then, the lion, who had for a long time been at war with a wild bull, called out for the dolphin to come and help him. The dolphin tried to leave the water but failed to do so. The lion accused him of betraying him.

But the dolphin replied:

'Don't blame me. Blame Mother Nature [*physis*]. For although she has made me aquatic, she has not allowed me to walk on the land.'

This shows that we too, when we contract alliances, ought to do so with people who can really come to our aid in times of danger.

203

The Lion and the Wild Boar

In summer, when the heat brings on thirst, a lion and a wild boar went to drink at a little spring. They argued about who should drink first, and the quarrel escalated into a life-and-death struggle.

But, stopping for a moment to catch their breath in the midst of their combat, they noticed some vultures waiting nearby to devour whichever one fell first. So, putting aside their hostility, they said:

'It would be better to become friends than serve as food for vultures and ravens.'

It is better to put an end to quarrels and rivalries, for otherwise all parties will suffer.

204

The Lion and the Hare

A lion, having come across a sleeping hare, was about to eat it. But, just at that moment, he caught sight of a deer. So he left the hare and gave chase to the deer. The hare, awoken by the noise, took flight.

The lion, having followed the deer for some distance without being able to catch up, went back for the hare. But he found that it had gone.

'It serves me right,' he said. 'I forfeited the meal I had right at hand for the hope of a better catch.'

Thus, at times men, instead of being content with moderate profits, pursue fantastic prospects and, in so doing, foolishly let go of what they have in their hands.

205

The Lion, the Wolf
and the Fox

A very old lion lay ill in his cave. All of the animals came to pay their respects to their king except for the fox. The wolf, sensing an opportunity, accused the fox in front of the lion:

'The fox has no respect for you or your rule. That's why he hasn't even come to visit you.'

Just as the wolf was saying this, the fox arrived, and he overheard these words. Then the lion roared in rage at him, but the fox managed to say in his own defence:

'And who, of all those who have gathered here, has rendered Your Majesty as much service as I have done? For I have travelled far and wide asking physicians for a remedy for your illness, and I have found one.'

The lion demanded to know at once what cure he had found, and the fox said:

'It is necessary for you to flay a wolf alive, and then take his skin and wrap it around you while it is still warm.'

The wolf was ordered to be taken away immediately and flayed alive. As he was carried off, the fox turned to him with a smile and said:

'You should have spoken well of me to His Majesty rather than ill.'

This fable shows that if you speak ill of someone, you yourself will fall into a trap.

206

The Lion and the Mouse Who
Returned a Kindness

Once, a lion was asleep and a mouse ran all along his body. The lion woke up with a start, seized the mouse and was about to eat him, when the mouse begged him to spare his life, promising that he would repay the favour.

The lion was so amused at this that he let the little fellow go.

Not very long afterwards, the mouse was able to return the favour. For, as a matter of fact, some hunters caught the lion and tied him to a tree with a rope. The mouse heard him groaning, ran up and gnawed through the rope until the lion was free.

'You see?' squeaked the mouse. 'Not long ago you mocked me when I said I would return your favour. But now you can see that even mice are grateful!'

This fable shows how, through the changes of fortune, the strong can come to depend on the weak.

NOTE: A version of this fable occurs in the Indian fable collection, the *Pañcatantra*, in the 'Winning of Friends' section (169), only there it is a large number of mice who gnawed the ropes tying the king-elephant in a trap and set him free. The probability is that the Indian version is an adaptation of the Greek fable done after the time of Alexander the Great; see footnotes to Fables 71 and 267.

207

The Lion and the Wild Ass

A lion and a wild ass entered into an agreement to hunt wild beasts together. The lion was to use his great strength, while the ass would make use of his greater speed. When they had taken a certain number of animals, the lion divided up the spoils into three portions.

'I'll take the first share because I am the king,' he said.

'The second share will be mine because I have been your partner in the chase,' he said.

'As for the third share,' he said to the wild ass, 'this share will be a great source of harm to you, believe me, if you do not yield it up to me. And, by the way, get lost!'

It is suitable always to calculate your own strength, and not to enter into an alliance with people stronger than yourself. ·

NOTE: This and the next two fables all ignore the obvious fact that the ass is not a carnivore and hence would not be interested in eating the animals caught. This leads to the supposition that the wild ass is a substitute for another animal, a carnivore which could run faster than a lion, in the original versions. See discussion in the Introduction.

208

The Lion and the Ass
Hunting Together

The lion and the ass, having a pact between them, were out together hunting. Arriving at a cave where there were wild goats, the lion posted himself at the entrance to lie in wait for them to leave, while the ass went inside and started leaping about and braying in their midst to make them flee.

When the lion had taken the largest of the wild goats, the ass came out and asked him if he hadn't bravely fought and pushed the goats outside.

The lion replied: 'I can assure you that even I would have been scared to death, if I hadn't know that you were an ass.'

Thus, people who boast in front of those who know them deservedly lend themselves to mockery.

209

The Lion, the Ass
and the Fox

The lion, the ass and the fox, having made an agreement together, went off hunting for game. When they had taken plenty of game, the lion asked the ass to divide the spoils between them. The ass divided the food into three equal parts and invited the lion to choose his portion. The lion became enraged, pounced on the ass and devoured him.

Then the lion asked the fox to divide the spoils. The fox took all that they had accumulated and gathered it into one large heap, retaining only the tiniest possible morsel for himself. He then invited the lion to choose.

The lion then said:

'Well, my good fellow, who taught you to divide so well? You are excellent at it.'

The fox replied:

'I learned this technique from the ass's misfortune.'

This fable shows that we learn from the misfortunes of others.

The Lion, Prometheus and the Elephant

The lion was always complaining to Prometheus. Without doubt, Prometheus had made him large and handsome, he had armed him with a mouth full of teeth, equipped him with claws and made him stronger than all the other animals. 'But, Prometheus,' said the lion, 'I am absolutely terrified of cockerels!'

Prometheus said:

'How can you accuse me so readily? I've given you all the qualities which I have myself. Your courage never fails you. Except in this one instance.'

'Oh, I know, I know,' the lion groaned. 'I feel such a fool. I'm such a hopeless coward. Oh, I wish I could just die, I'm so ashamed!'

But, just as he was in that frame of mind, the lion saw an elephant nearby and went over to have a chat with him about this and that. As they were talking, the lion noticed that the elephant kept twitching his ears.

'What's wrong?' asked the lion. 'Can't you keep your ears still for one moment?'

At that very moment a gnat settled on the head of the elephant.

'Oh, my God!' said the elephant. 'Do you see that? There, that little buzzing insect, there! If it were to get into my ears, why, I'd be finished. That would be the end of me. I'd die, you know!'

'Well,' said the lion to himself, 'I don't feel so bad any more. And to think I was wishing myself dead for shame! In fact, I'm big and strong and much better off than the elephant, since a cockerel is much more frightening than a gnat!'

One sees that the gnat is strong enough to make even an elephant fearful.

211

The Lion and the Bull

A lion wanted to hunt down a bull, so he decided to use a trick to try to get hold of him. He told him that he had sacrificed a sheep and he invited the bull to the feast, his intention being to kill him when he was reclining on his side to eat. The bull accepted the invitation but, seeing the huge spits and giant cauldrons – but no sheep – he departed without saying a word. The lion reproached him as to why, having suffered no harm, he left without reason.

'Oh, I have my reasons,' said the bull. 'I see no sign of your having slaughtered a sheep but I do see, very plainly, that you have made every preparation for dining on beef.'

This fable shows that you should trust your own eyes rather than sweet words and reassurances.

212

The Raging Lion and the Stag

A lion was enraged and a stag, who saw him from the forest, called out:

'Woe betide us! What won't this lion do in his fury, when he was already intolerable in a calm frame of mind!'

Avoid hotheaded men who are accustomed to doing harm when they come to power.

213

The Lion Who Was Afraid of a Mouse, and the Fox

There was a lion lying asleep one day when a mouse ran all the way up his body. The lion awoke with a start and rolled over and over, trying to find out what or who it was that had attacked him. A fox, who had seen all this, rebuked him for being afraid – he, a lion, afraid of a mouse! To which the lion replied:

'It isn't that I was afraid of the mouse, but I was most surprised that there was anyone at all who could be so bold as to run along the body of a sleeping lion.'

This fable shows that wise men don't ignore even the little things.

214

The Bandit and the
Mulberry Tree

A bandit, who had killed a man on the road, saw that he was being pursued by some people who happened to be nearby. So he abandoned his bloodstained victim and fled. But some travellers who were coming in the opposite direction asked him what had made his hands so stained. He said he had just climbed down from a mulberry tree. When he said this, the people who were pursuing him caught up with him, seized him and hung him from a nearby mulberry tree. And the tree said to him:

'I am not sorry to assist with your punishment. You are the one who committed the murder, and yet you wiped the blood on me.'

Even naturally good men, when they see themselves slandered, do not hesitate to show spite towards those who have slandered them.

215

The Wolves and the Dogs
at War

One day, enmity broke out between the dogs and the wolves. The dogs elected a Greek to be their general. But he was in no hurry to engage in battle, despite the violent intimidation of the wolves. 'Understand,' he said to them, 'why I deliberately put off engagement. It is because one must always take counsel before acting. The wolves, on the one hand, are all of the same race, all of the same colour. But our soldiers have very varied habits, and each one is proud of his own country. Even their colours are not uniform: some are black, some russett, and others white or ash-grey. How can I lead into battle those who are not in harmony and who are all dissimilar?'

In all armies it is unity of will and purpose which assures victory over the enemy.

NOTE: The reference to the dogs being proud of their own countries refers to the ancient Greek habit of calling dogs by the names of the countries or regions in which they were customarily bred, such as Molossian or Laconian hounds or Maltese terriers. Different breeds of dogs were thus named after different countries in common parlance, so that if one spoke of them all one seemed to be talking of many countries.

216

The Dogs Reconciled with the Wolves

The wolves said to the dogs: 'Why, when you are so like us in all respects, don't we come to some brotherly understanding? For there is no difference between us except our ways of thinking. We live in freedom; you submit and are enslaved by man and endure his blows. You wear collars and you watch over their flocks, and when your masters eat, all they throw to you are some bones. But take our word for it, if you hand over the flocks to us we can all club together and gorge our appetites jointly.'

The dogs were sympathetic to this proposal, so the wolves, making their way inside the sheepfold, tore the dogs to pieces.

Such is the reward that traitors who betray their fatherland deserve.

217

The Wolves and the Sheep

Some wolves were trying to surprise a flock of sheep. Unable to be masters of the situation because of the dogs which were guarding them, they resolved to use a ruse to reach their desired end: they sent some delegates to ask the sheep to give up their dogs. It was the dogs, they said, who created the bad blood between them. One only had to surrender the dogs and peace would reign between them. The sheep, not foreseeing what would happen, gave up the dogs. And the wolves, being in control of the situation, easily slaughtered the sheep who were no longer guarded.

This is the case with states: those who easily surrender up their orators cannot doubt that they will very soon be subjugated by their enemies.

218

The Wolves, the Sheep and the Ram

The wolves sent some envoys to the sheep, offering to make a lasting peace with them if they surrendered up their dogs to be put to death. The stupid sheep agreed to do it. But an old ram exclaimed:

'How should I accept that idea and live with you when, even when we were guarded by the dogs, it was impossible for me to graze in safety?'

We must not part with that which assures our safety, in making faith with our irreconcilable enemies.

219

The Wolf Proud of His Shadow, and the Lion

One day a wolf was wandering in some uninhabited regions at the hour when the sun sinks low down towards the horizon. Seeing his elongated shadow, he said:

'Look at that! With my stature, should I fear the lion? With such an immense size, should I not become the king of all the animals?'

And as he was fully given up to pride with this thought, a lion of great strength suddenly leapt upon him and devoured him.

The wolf changed his opinion and cried:

'Presumption brings us misfortune.'

220

The Wolf and the Goat

A wolf espied a nanny-goat grazing above a cave on a sheer cliff-face. Unable to reach her, he urged her to come down. For she could, he said, inadvertently fall. Furthermore, the meadow down below, where he was standing, was much better for pasture, for the grass there was lush. But the goat replied:

'It's not for my benefit that you summon me to that pasture; it is because it is *you* who have nothing to eat.'

Thus, when cunning scoundrels exert their wickedness among people whom they know, they gain nothing by their machinations.

221

The Wolf and the Lamb

A wolf saw a lamb drinking at a stream and wanted to devise a suitable pretext for devouring it. So, although he was himself upstream, he accused the lamb of muddying the water and preventing him from drinking. The lamb replied that he only drank with the tip of his tongue and that, besides, being downstream he couldn't muddy the water upstream. The wolf's stratagem having collapsed, he replied:

'But last year you insulted my father.'

'I wasn't even born then,' replied the lamb.

So the wolf resumed:

'Whatever you say to justify yourself, I will eat you all the same.'

This fable shows that when some people decide upon doing harm, the fairest defence has no effect whatever.

222

The Wolf and the Young Lamb
Taking Refuge in a Temple

A wolf pursued a young lamb, who took refuge in a temple. The wolf called out to it and said that the sacrificer would offer it up to the god if he found the lamb there. But the lamb replied:

'Ah well! I would prefer to be a victim of a god than to die by your hand.'

This fable shows that if one is being driven towards death, it is better to die with honour.

223

The Wolf and the Old Woman

A hungry wolf was prowling in search of food. Coming to a certain place, he heard a child crying and an old woman who was saying to it:

'Don't cry any more, or else I will give you to the wolf at once!'

The wolf thought that the old woman meant it, so he stopped and waited for a long time. When evening fell he again heard the old woman cuddling the little one, saying to it:

'If the wolf comes here, my child, we will kill him.'

After hearing these words, the wolf went on his way, saying:

'In this farm they say one thing and do another.'

This fable addresses itself to people who do not match their words with their deeds.

224

The Wolf and the Heron

A wolf swallowed a bone and looked everywhere for relief from his predicament. He met a heron who, for a certain fee, agreed to retrieve the bone. So the heron lowered his head into the wolf's throat, pulled out the bone, and then claimed his promised fee.

'Listen, pal!' replied the wolf. 'Isn't it enough to have pulled your head safe and sound from a wolf's throat? What more do you want?'

This fable shows that the most we can expect from bad people is that they won't commit an injury against us in addition to their lack of gratitude.

225

The Wolf and the Horse

A wolf crossed an arable field [*aroura*] and discovered that it contained barley. As he couldn't eat it, he left it and went on his way. Soon after he met a horse, whom he led to the field, telling him he had found some barley.

The wolf said:

'Rather than eat it myself, I decided to watch over it for you instead. For I very much enjoy the sound of your munching.'

The horse replied:

'Ha! My friend, if wolves could eat barley for their dinner, you would never have preferred the use of your ears to the filling of your stomach!'

This fable shows that those who are naturally wicked, even when they pride themselves on being good, are not actually believed.

226

The Wolf and the Dog

A wolf saw a huge dog wearing a large wooden restraining-collar and asked him:

'Who has chained you up and fed you like that?'

'A hunter,' replied the dog.

'Ah, God preserve wolves from him, as much as from hunger and a heavy restraining-collar!'

This fable shows that in misfortune one doesn't even have the pleasures of the stomach.

NOTE: In ancient Greece large or unruly dogs were restrained by a heavy wooden collar called a *kloios*. The meaning of the fable depends upon knowing about this obsolete object.

227

The Wolf and the Lion

One day, a wolf seized a sheep from a flock and carried it to his lair. But, on his way, a lion crossed his path and took the sheep from him. The wolf remained at a safe distance but complained to the lion:

'You have no right to take my property!'

The lion said to the wolf mockingly:

'You came by it honestly yourself, as a gift from a friend, no doubt?'

Insatiable plunderers and thieves who fall out among themselves when they meet with a setback can learn from this story.

228

The Wolf and the Ass

A wolf became chief over the other wolves and established some general laws to the effect that whatever was caught by hunting would be shared communally. By that means, the wolves would never again be reduced to a shortage of food and thus to eating one another.

But an ass came forward and, shaking his mane, said:

'The wolf has been inspired by a noble idea. But what about your catch of yesterday which you have concealed in your lair? Bring it out and share it with the community.' The wolf, disconcerted, abolished his laws.

Those who seem to legislate according to justice cannot even abide by the rules which they themselves have established and decreed.

229

The Wolf and the Shepherd

A wolf followed a flock of sheep without doing them any harm. At first the shepherd was fearful of it as an enemy and watched it nervously. But, as the wolf kept on following without making any attempt to harm them, he began to look upon it as more of a guardian than an enemy to be wary of. As he needed to go into town one day, he left the sheep with the wolf in attendance. The wolf, seeing his opportunity, hurled himself at the sheep and tore most of them to pieces. When the shepherd returned and saw the lost sheep he cried out:

'It serves me right. How could I have entrusted my sheep to a wolf?'

It is the same with men: when you entrust valuables to greedy people it is natural that you will lose things.

230

The Satisfied Wolf
and the Ewe

A wolf, well-gorged with food, saw a ewe lying on her back on the ground, unable to right herself. Realizing that she had collapsed from fright, he approached her and reassured her. He promised that if she would utter three truths he would leave her alone. So the ewe began by telling him she would like not to have to meet him again, or failing that she would like him to go blind, and thirdly she wished 'that wicked wolves would meet violent deaths so that we would suffer no more harm from you and you would make no more war against us'. The wolf acknowledged her veracity and left her to go her own way.

This fable shows that often truth has this effect on one's enemies.

231

The Injured Wolf
and the Ewe

A wolf, bitten and injured by some dogs, had fallen to the ground. As he was in no state to hunt for food, he espied a ewe and begged her to fetch him a drink from the nearby stream:

'If you give me something to drink I will find myself something to eat,' said the wolf.

'But if I give you something to drink,' replied the ewe, 'it is I who will make you a meal.'

This fable is aimed at the wrongdoer who lays a hypocritical trap.

232

The Lamp

Intoxicated with oil, a lamp threw out a vivid light, boasting that it was more brilliant than the sun. But a gust of wind blew up and it was extinguished instantly. Someone relit it and said:

'Light up, lamp, and be assured that the light of the stars is never eclipsed.'

You mustn't be dazzled by pride when you are held in high repute, for all that is acquired is extraneous to us.

233

The Diviner

A diviner was sitting plying his trade in the agora. Suddenly, someone rushed up to him and said that the front door of his house was wide open and the contents gone. The diviner leapt up in consternation and ran home, gasping to see what had happened. A passer-by who saw him running called out:

'Hey there! You who pride yourself on foretelling the future for others! Can't you foresee what will happen to yourself?'

One could apply this fable to people who order their own lives woefully but who dabble in controlling affairs which are not their concern.

234

The Bees and Zeus

Begrudging the honey they gave to men, the bees went to Zeus to ask him to give them the power to kill with their stings anyone approaching their honeycombs. Indignant at their envy, Zeus condemned the bees to lose their sting-barbs every time they stung someone, and to die as a result.

This fable is applicable to those who suffer as a result of their own envy.

235

The Beekeeper

A man broke into a beekeeper's abode and, in his absence, stole some honey and honeycombs. When the beekeeper returned and saw the empty hives he stopped to examine them. But the bees, flying back home from foraging and finding him there, attacked him and stung him terribly.

'Wretched creatures,' he exclaimed, 'you let the person who stole your combs escape with impunity and you mercilessly persecute me, who takes care of you!'

Thus, it often happens that, through ignorance, we are not on guard against our enemies and that we drive off our friends and hold them in suspicion.

236

The Begging Priests of Cybele

Some begging priests had an ass which carried their possessions from place to place. Now, one day, the ass dropped down dead from exhaustion. So they skinned it, made kettledrums [*tympana*] from its skin, and thus continued to make use of it. Then, later on, they met another group of begging priests who asked them where their ass was.

'Oh, he is dead,' they replied, 'but he gets just as many blows as he did when he was alive.'

Thus, sometimes even when servants are freed from slavery they are not necessarily rid of the burdens of servitude.

NOTE: The *tympanon* was a kind of kettledrum especially used for the worship of the goddess Cybele and the god Bacchus. The begging priests of Cybele were known as the *Mēnagyrtai*, which is the actual title of this fable in Greek.

237

The Mice and the House-ferrets

The mice and the house-ferrets were at war. Now the mice, always seeing themselves beaten, convened a committee, because they imagined that it must be the lack of a leader which caused their setbacks. They elected some generals by raising their hands. Now, the new generals wanted to be distinguished from the ordinary soldiers, so they fashioned some horns and fastened them to their heads. The battle got under way and it happened that the army of the mice was defeated by the house-ferrets. The soldiers fled towards their holes, into which they escaped easily. But the generals, not being able to enter because of their horns getting stuck, were caught and devoured.

Thus, vainglory is often a cause of misfortune.

238

The Fly

A fly had fallen into an earthen pot [*chytros*] full of boiled meat. On the verge of drowning in the broth [*zōmos*], she said to herself:

'I've eaten, I've drunk, I've had a bath. Death can come. It doesn't matter to me.'

This fable shows that people easily surrender to death when it comes without any suffering.

239

The Flies

Some flies had found some spilled honey in a cellar and started to eat it. It was such a sweet feast that they couldn't stop. But their feet became stuck to the spot so that they couldn't take flight. And, as they began to suffocate, they said:

'How wretched we are! We are dying for a moment's pleasure.'

Gluttony is often the cause of much harm.

240

The Ant

Once upon a time, the ant used to be human – a farmer who, not content with his own yield, kept an envious eye on his neighbour's harvest and stole it. Zeus was angered by his greed and changed him into the insect that we call an ant. But, even though his body was altered, his character was not. To this day he still traverses the fields collecting other people's wheat and barley and storing it up for himself.

This fable shows that even a severe punishment doesn't change people who, by nature, are bad characters.

241

The Ant and the Scarab Beetle

All summer an ant roamed the countryside gathering up grains of wheat and barley and storing them up for winter. Seeing this, a scarab beetle expressed surprise that she was working so hard at the time of year when most other animals rested from their labours and had a holiday. At the time the ant didn't reply. But when winter had come and rain soaked the dung, the scarab beetle was hungry. She asked the ant to lend her a bit of food. Then the ant replied:

'Oh, beetle! If you had worked when I took the trouble to, instead of mocking me, you would have plenty of food now too.'

Similarly, in times of abundance we should plan ahead lest we suffer distress when times change.

NOTE: Scarab beetles were sacred in Egypt. See also Fables 4 and 149.

242

The Ant and the Pigeon

A thirsty ant went down to a spring to drink but was caught by the flow of water coming from it and was about to be swept away. Seeing this, a pigeon broke a twig from a nearby tree and threw it into the water. The ant clambered on to it and was saved.

While this was going on, a fowler came along with his limed twigs ready to catch the pigeon. The ant saw what was happening and bit the man's foot, so that the pain made him suddenly throw down the twigs, and the pigeon flew off.

This fable shows that one good turn deserves another.

243

The Field Mouse and
the Town Mouse

A field mouse had a town mouse for a friend. The field mouse invited the town mouse to dinner in the country. When he saw that there was only barley and corn to eat, the town mouse said:

'Do you know, my friend, that you live like an ant? I, on the other hand, have an abundance of good things. Come home with me and I will share it all with you.'

So they set off together. The house mouse showed his friend some beans and bread-flour, together with some dates, a cheese, honey and fruit. And the field mouse was filled with wonder and blessed him with all his heart, cursing his own lot. Just as they were preparing to start their meal, a man suddenly opened the door. Alarmed by the noise, the mice rushed fearfully into the crevices.

Then, as they crept out again to taste some dried figs, someone else came into the room and started looking for something. So they again rushed down the holes to hide. Then the field mouse, forgetting his hunger, sighed, and said to his friend:

'Farewell, my friend. You can eat your fill and be glad of heart, but at the price of a thousand fears and dangers. I, poor little thing, will go on living by nibbling barley and corn without fear or suspicion of anyone.'

This fable shows that one should:

> *Live simply and free from passion*
> *Instead of luxuriously in fear and dread.*

NOTE: This fable, like several others, is in verse, but we have only rendered the moral in verse. Horace also did a version of this fable in *Satires* (II, 6, 79–117); it is a witty verse tale told to conclude Satire 6 of Book II, which hints that the story was a popular one in Rome at that time. Fontaine's fable of 'The Town Mouse and the Country Mouse' derives only its title from Aesop and differs otherwise.

244

The Mouse and the Frog

A land mouse struck up an ill-fated friendship with a frog. One day, the frog, who had evil intentions, tied the paw of the mouse to his own foot. At first they leapt over the ground to eat some corn. Then they approached the edge of the pond. Then the frog dragged the mouse to the bottom, while playing about in the water making his '*brekekekex*' noises. And the unfortunate mouse, bloated with the water, was drowned. But his body floated to the surface, attached to the foot of the frog. A kite spotted it, swooped down and seized it with his talons, and the frog, tied to the mouse, soon followed – and served also to provide a dinner for the kite.

Even death can avenge itself; for divine justice observes everything, and restores the equal proportions of her balance beam.

NOTE: The use of the word *brekekekex* to imitate the croaking of frogs is best known from its use in the play *The Frogs* by Aristophanes. A mouse drowned as a result of an ill-fated friendship with a frog also features in the epic parody, *Battle of the Frogs and Mice* (90), and then leads to warfare between the two species. There, in true Aesopic fashion, the drowning mouse is thus described: 'Then, at the last, as he was dying, he uttered these words . . .' The mock-epic is very funny, though some who have little sense of humour have not seen that. Although often attributed to Homer, Suda (formerly called by scholars Suidas) maintains that it was actually written by Pigres of Caria circa 480 BC. Certainly, there are connections between the mock-epic and the fable. B. E. Perry thinks that Demetrius of Phalerum made a fable from the mock-epic, but the apparent parody by the mock-epic of an Aesopic death-speech indicates that the mock-epic was actually making fun of a pre-existing fable, which thus may be an actual work of Aesop, considering the antiquity of the parody by Pigres.

245

The Castaway and the Sea

A castaway, flung on to the shore, slept from exhaustion. But it wasn't long before he woke and, seeing the sea, reproached her for seducing men with her tranquil air. For then, when she had them in her watery grip, she became wild and caused them to perish. The sea, having taken the form of a woman, said to him:

'But, my friend, it's not up to me. You should instead reproach the winds. For I am naturally as you see me now. It's the winds who, falling on me without a moment's warning, swell me and make me wild.'

Similarly, we ought not to be blamed for being the originators of an injustice when it has been carried out on the order of others, but rather blame should fall on those who have authority over us.

246

The Young Men and
the Butcher

Two young men were buying meat from the same meat stall. While the butcher's back was turned one of the youths grabbed some cheap bits of ears, trotters and so forth, and thrust them into the loose pocket-fold of the garment of the other. When the butcher turned round he looked for the morsels and accused the youths. But the one who had taken them swore he hadn't got them and the one who had them swore he hadn't taken them. Seeing through their false statements, the butcher said:

'You can get away with a false oath to me but you certainly won't escape the notice of the gods.'

This fable shows that, however persuasive the sophistries by which they are made, false oaths are still impious.

NOTE: There is no direct English translation for the word *akrokōlion*, which refers collectively to the extremities of an animal's body such as ears, trotters and snout.

247

The Fawn and the Stag

One day, a fawn said to the stag:

'Father, you are so much bigger and faster than the dogs and you have such splendid antlers to defend yourself. So why do you always run away from them?'

The stag replied with a laugh:

'It's true, my child, what you say, but one thing is certain: whenever I hear the hounds baying I make a dash for it even though I don't know where I am fleeing.'

This fable shows that no amount of exhortation can reassure the faint-hearted.

248

The Young Wastrel and the Swallow

Having squandered his inheritance, a young wastrel possessed only his cloak. He noticed a swallow who had arrived early, so, thinking that summer had come, he took off his cloak and sold that too. But wintery weather was still to come. It grew very cold. He was out walking one day when he came across the swallow, frozen to death. He said:

'Miserable wretch! You've ruined us both at once.'

This fable shows that it is always dangerous to do things at the wrong moment.

249

The Sick Man and the Doctor

A sick man, questioned about his health by the doctor, replied that he was sweating heavily.

'That is good,' said the doctor.

Then he asked him the next time how he was feeling, and the patient said he had been shivering so much he was badly shaken up.

'That's also good,' said the doctor.

Then he called on the man a third time and asked how he was. He replied that he had had diarrhoea.

'That's good too,' said the doctor, and went on his way.

Then one of the sick man's parents came to visit him and asked how he was.

'I'm dying of good symptoms,' he replied.

So it is sometimes: judging things by appearances, our neighbours assume we are happy with the things which are, in fact, causing us the most grief.

250

The Bat, the Bramble
and the Gull

The bat, the bramble and the gull met up with the intention of doing a bit of trading together. The bat went out and borrowed some money to fund the enterprise, the bramble contributed a lot of cloth to be sold and the gull brought a large supply of copper to sell. Then they set sail to go trading, but a violent storm arose which capsized their ship and all the cargo was lost. They were able to save nothing but themselves from the shipwreck.

Ever since that time, the gull has searched the seashore to see if any of his copper might be washed up somewhere, the bat, fearing his creditors, dare not go out by day and only feeds at night, and the bramble clutches the clothes of all those who pass by, hoping to recognize a familiar piece of material.

This fable shows that we always return to those things in which we have a stake.

251

The Bat and the House-ferrets

A bat fell to the ground and was caught by a house-ferret. Realizing that she was on the point of being killed, she begged for her life. The house-ferret said to her that she couldn't let her go, for ferrets were supposed to be natural enemies to all birds. The bat replied that she herself was not a bird, but a mouse. She managed to extricate herself from her danger by this means.

Eventually, falling a second time, the bat was caught by another house-ferret. Again she pleaded to the ferret not to eat her. The second ferret declared that she absolutely detested all mice. But the bat positively affirmed that she was not a mouse but a bat. And so she was released again.

And that was how she saved herself from death twice by a mere change of name.

This fable shows that it is not always necessary to confine ourselves to the same tactics. But, on the contrary, if we are adaptable to circumstances we can better escape danger.

252

The Logs and the Olive

Once the logs were consulting among themselves to elect a king. They asked the olive:

'Reign over us.'

The olive tree replied:

'What? Give up my oily liquor which is so highly prized by god and man to go and reign over the logs?'

And so the logs asked the fig:

'Come and reign over us.'

But the fig replied similarly:

'What? Relinquish the sweetness of my delicious fruit to go and reign over the logs?'

So the logs urged the thornbush:

'Come and reign over us.'

And the thorn replied:

'If you were really to anoint me king over you, you would have to take shelter beneath me. Otherwise the flames from my brushwood [a usual tinder] would escape and devour the cedars of Lebanon.'

NOTE: The word *xylon* means 'firewood' or 'log' but Professor Chambry mistranslated it as *arbre*, 'tree', because he missed the joke, as have all other translators known to us. This fable appears in the Bible in the Book of Judges (ix. 8), and both the King James translation and the *New English Bible* mention trees rather than logs; we have not consulted the Septuagint, as that is taking a footnote too far, nor can we read Hebrew.

The Greek fable appears to have been taken into the Bible, rather than the other way round. Our reasons for believing this are that the fable only really makes sense if we realize that it is about logs rather than trees, and the misunderstanding which led to people thinking it was about trees rather than logs obviously took place prior to the interpolation of the story into the Book of Judges, where the fable is put into the mouth of Jotham as a way for him to say 'may fire come out of Abimelech'. Apart from the mistranslation of *xylon* as 'tree', the text of the Aesop fable and the text found in the Bible are extraordinarily close, indicating a borrowing not by any historical Jotham, whose speeches were remembered, but by a very literary writer of the Book of Judges who had a Greek text before him and who, like Professor Chambry, entirely missed the joke. The wry humour of the fable, so typical of the Aesopic material, is not only unlike the earnest tone so typical of the Bible, but also the humour of the fable is actually entirely overlooked by the serious-minded author of the Book of Judges.

It seems to us utterly impossible that the fable could have originated in the Bible and drifted into the Aesop collections from there, since that would mean an inconceivable injection of humour and specific meaning not present in the Bible; such processes do not happen in reverse, nor does water run uphill. What has happened is that a funny fable was misinterpreted by a Hebrew author whose Greek was a bit rusty, and borrowed for a wholly non-funny purpose of a man complaining that his family have been murdered – just about the most incongruous context imaginable. Possibly the reason why the author of the Book of Judges took to the fable was that it mentioned the cedars of Lebanon, which were, of course, just as famous in Greece as they were in Israel; he must have thought that the idea of fire burning up the cedars of Lebanon was a very powerful image for fire consuming Abimelech. But, certainly, humour cannot be pumped into a humourless fable afterwards, it has got to be there to start with and become lost in transition.

What this means for dating we cannot say, not being Biblical scholars and having no idea when the Book of Judges may have been written, or indeed whether the fable may have been a later addition to the oldest manuscript, which we believe to be the Septuagint, which, as it was in Greek, might mean the fable was added at that stage by some earnest Alexandrian. In that case there is no need for the fable to be particularly ancient; it could be Hellenistic. Let us also not lose sight of the fact that the idea of the logs seeking to elect a king, in the light of all the other fables where various animals and plants seek kings, is a joke which was probably thought to be hysterically funny at the time, especially in the context of the Aesop collections; in other words, the fable may well have been composed as a satirical addition to the collection purely in a spirit of fun.

253

The Woodcutter and Hermes

A woodcutter who was chopping wood on the banks of a river had lost his axe. Not knowing what to do, he sat himself down on the bank and wept. The god Hermes, learning the cause of his distress, took pity on him. Hermes plunged into the river, brought out a golden axe and asked the woodcutter if this were the one which he had lost. The man said, no, that wasn't the one. So Hermes dived back in again and this time he produced a silver axe. But the woodcutter said, no, that wasn't his axe either.

Hermes plunged in a third time and brought him his own axe. The man said, yes, indeed, this was the very axe which he had lost.

Then Hermes, charmed by his honesty, gave him all three.

Returning to his friends, the woodcutter told them about his adventure. One of them took it into his head to get himself some axes as well. So he set off for the riverbank, threw his axe into the current deliberately and then sat down in tears. Then Hermes appeared to him also and, learning the cause of his tears, he dived in and brought him too a golden axe, asking if it were the one which he had lost.

The man, all joyful, cried out: 'Yes! It is indeed the one!'

But the god, horrified at such effrontery, not only withheld the golden axe but didn't return the man's own.

This fable shows that the gods favour honest people but are hostile to the dishonest.

NOTE: This fable would appear to be based upon an initiatory ritual from some mystery religion, and the motif of the valuable gold or silver weapon fetched by a god from beneath the water derives from the same sources as the more familiar traditions of the 'Lady of the Lake', Excalibur and the Ring of the Niebelungen. As for the axe, it had particularly sacred significance in Minoan times and its sacred associations go back into the Stone Age cultures.

254

The Travellers and the Bear

Two friends were travelling along the same path together when a bear suddenly appeared. One of them quickly climbed up a tree and hid himself there. The other, who was about to be caught, threw himself down on the ground and feigned death. The bear sniffed him all over with his muzzle, but the man held his breath. For it is said that a bear will not touch a corpse.

When the bear had gone away, the man hiding in the tree came down and asked his friend what the bear had whispered in his ear.

The other replied: 'Not to travel in future with friends who slip away when there is danger.'

This fable shows that when danger threatens, true friends will face it.

NOTE: Feigning death and remaining absolutely motionless while being sniffed by a dangerous animal is a common way of surviving in such a harrowing situation; W. H. Hudson once saved his life by doing this when attacked by a bull on the open Argentine pampas, and there are many similar stories of people who have saved themselves in this way from attacks by ferocious creatures of various kinds. The fable thus preserves an accurate and timeless tradition which must have been better known in the Stone Age when the beasts were more dangerous and more plentiful. As is so typical of the Aesopic material, the situation has been turned to advantage to make a joke.

255

The Travellers and the Raven

Some people, travelling on business, came across a one-eyed raven. They turned to look at it and one of them advised that they retrace their steps, it being a bad omen in his opinion. But another of the men spoke up:

'How can this bird predict the future for us when he couldn't predict his own and avoid the loss of his eye?'

Likewise, people who are blinded by their own interests are poorly qualified to give counsel to their neighbours.

NOTE: One should interpret this fable in the context of knowing that bird augury was a very common superstition of the time, just as popular as astrology columns in the newspapers are today; but, in the case of bird augury, it had the advantage of complete sanction by the official religion. In fact, at a later date in Rome, the orator Cicero was official Augur for the Roman State.

256

The Travellers and the Axe

Two men were travelling together. One of them found an axe along the way and he said to his companion:

'We've found an axe.'

'Don't say we have found, say you have found,' said the other man.

Soon afterwards they were joined by the men who had lost the axe, and the one who had it, seeing that they were about to chase him, said:

'We are lost!'

'Don't say we are lost,' replied his companion, 'but "I am lost." For since you found the axe you haven't granted me half of your lucky find.'

This fable shows that if you are not willing to share good luck with a friend, you should not expect him to stand by you in misfortune.

257

The Travellers and the Plane Tree

One summer, in the heat of the midday sun, two weary travellers stretched out under the shady branches of a plane tree to rest. Looking up into the tree, they agreed:

'Here is a tree that is sterile and useless to man.'

The plane tree answered:

'Ungrateful wretches, at the very same time that you are enjoying my benefits you accuse me of being sterile and useless.'

Some people are like this: some are so unlucky that even though they are good to their neighbours, they can't make them believe in their benevolence.

258

The Travellers and the Brushwood

Trudging along a cliff path, some travellers came to a high point. In the distance they could see some brushwood floating on the sea. They mistook it for a warship and therefore waited, thinking it would land. Then the brushwood, pushed by the wind, came nearer and they no longer thought it was a warship but a cargo ship. Later on, when they got to the beach, they realized that it was only a clump of brushwood. And they agreed:

'What fools we were to wait for something that was nothing!'

This fable shows that some people who appear formidable because they are strangers reveal at the first test that they are nonentities.

259

The Traveller and Truth

Travelling through a desert, a man came upon a solitary woman
who kept her eyes lowered.

'Who are you?' he asked.

'I am Truth [*Alētheia*],' she replied.

'And why have you left the town and come to live in the desert?'
She replied:

'Because, in days gone by, lies were only known to a few men,
but now they are everywhere – with everyone you speak to.'

Life will be evil and painful for men while lies prevail over truth.

260

The Traveller and Hermes

A traveller who had a long journey to make made a vow to the god
Hermes that, if he should arrive safely, he would consecrate to the
god half of anything he found along the way. As it happened, he
found on the journey a carrying-pouch which contained some
almonds and some dates. When he saw this, he picked it up, imagining
it to be full of money. He shook out the contents and ate them.
Then he took the shells of the almonds and the stones of the dates
and placed them on an altar, saying:

'Oh, Hermes, I have kept my vow. For I have shared with you
the outside and the inside of that which I have found.'

*This fable applies to the miser who, through greed, uses trickery even with
the gods.*

261

The Traveller and Chance

A man was worn out after a long journey, so he threw himself down beside a well and went to sleep. He would certainly have fallen in, but Chance [*Tychē*] appeared and woke him, saying:

'Hey, friend! If you had fallen down the well you wouldn't have blamed your own foolishness – you would have blamed me.'

Thus, plenty of people who meet with misfortune through their own fault blame it on the gods.

262

The Asses Appealing to Zeus

One day, the asses tired of suffering and carrying heavy burdens and they sent some representatives to Zeus, asking him to put a limit on their workload. Wanting to show them that this was impossible, Zeus told them that they would be delivered from their misery only when they could make a river from their piss. The asses took this reply seriously and, from that day until now, whenever they see ass piss anywhere they stop in their tracks to piss too.

This fable shows that one can do nothing to change one's destiny.

263

The Ass Bought in the Market

A man who intended to buy an ass took it on trial and led it to the manger to mix with his others. But the ass, turning its back on the others, went and stood beside the laziest and fattest of the lot. As it stood there and did nothing, the man put a halter on it and led it back to its owner. The owner asked the man if he had given it a fair trial, and he replied:

'I don't need any further trial. I am certain of what he's like because of the companion he chose from among the lot.'

This fable shows that people judge us by the company we keep.

NOTE: Professor Chambry gives this fable the title 'The Man who Bought an Ass'. But the original title does not mention the man.

264

The Wild Ass and the Domestic Ass

A wild ass which saw a domestic ass grazing in plenty of sunshine went up to it to compliment it on its plumpness and on the pasture which it enjoyed. But, moments later, he saw it loaded with a burden and followed by the ass-driver, who hit it with a club. So he called out to it:

'Oh, I don't congratulate you any more. For I can see that you pay a high price to enjoy your abundance.'

Thus, there is nothing to envy in advantage which is accompanied by danger and suffering.

265

The Ass Carrying Salt

An ass with a load of salt was crossing a stream. He slipped and fell into the water. Then the salt dissolved, and when he got up his load was lighter than before, so he was delighted. Another time, when he arrived at the bank of a stream with a load of sponges, he thought that if he fell into the water again when he got up the load would be lighter. So he slipped on purpose. But, of course, the sponges swelled up with the water and the ass was unable to get up again, so he drowned and perished.

Thus it is sometimes that people don't suspect that it is their own tricks which land them in disaster.

266

The Ass Carrying a Statue
of a God

An ass, who was carrying a statue of a god on its back, was being led into the town by a man. As the passers-by prostrated themselves in front of the statue, the ass imagined that it was he to whom they were making obeisance and, in his pride, he started to bray and refused to go any further. The ass-driver, guessing his thoughts, beat him with his club and said:

'Poor, brainless wretch! That really would be the limit, to see an ass adored by men.'

This fable shows that people who take an empty pride in the advantages of others become a laughing stock to those who know them.

NOTE: There is possibly more to this fable than meets the eye. There may be an intended ironical reference to the story written by Lucius of Patra about The Gold Ass, later written up in a famous book, *The Metamorphoses* or *Golden Ass*, by Apuleius, in the second century AD, and which is every bit as humorous as the Aesop fables.

267

The Ass Clothed in the Skin of a Lion, and the Fox

An ass who had clothed himself in the skin of a lion went about the countryside frightening all the animals. He encountered a fox and tried to frighten him also. But the fox, who had heard his voice before, said to him:

'You would have scared me too, there's no doubt about it, if I hadn't heard you bray.'

Thus, uneducated people who put on airs betray themselves by their longing to speak.

NOTE: A version of this fable is found in the 'Loss or Gains' section of the Indian *Pañcatantra* (44), but there a donkey is clothed in a tiger's skin by his owner so that he can browse in other people's barley fields safely and the farmers would be too frightened to drive him off. However, the donkey brays and the enraged farmers then kill him with stones, arrows and blows with wooden staves. This is probably an adaptation of the Greek fable done after the time of Alexander the Great; see notes to Fables 71 and 206.

268

The Ass Pronouncing
the Horse Happy

The ass discovered that the horse had plenty to eat and was well groomed, while he himself didn't even have enough litter, even though he was so willing to work. But there came a time of war: the horse had to carry a horseman armed from head to foot who urged him in every direction and even forced him into the midst of the enemy, where the horse was pierced with blows and slaughtered. On realizing this, the ass changed his mind and pitied the horse.

This fable shows that you shouldn't envy leaders or the rich, but think of the dangers to which they are exposed and resign yourself to poverty.

269

The Ass, the Cock
and the Lion

One day, an ass and a cockerel were feeding together when a lion attacked the ass. The cockerel let out a loud crow and the lion fled, for lions are afraid of the sound of a cock crowing.

The ass, imagining that the lion was fleeing because of him, did not hesitate to rush after him. When he had pursued the lion for about the distance where a cock's crow can no longer be heard, the lion turned round and devoured him. As he was dying, the ass brayed:

'What an unfortunate and stupid fellow I am! Why did I, who was not born to warlike parents, set out to fight?'

This fable shows that the enemy is often portrayed as of no consequence, but when we attack him he destroys us.

270

The Ass, the Fox
and the Lion

An ass and a fox made a pact to hunt together, and they sallied forth. But a lion appeared in their path. Hoping to save himself from this danger, the fox approached the lion and offered to entrap the ass on the lion's behalf. The lion promised that, if the fox did this, he would let him go free. So the fox led the ass towards a hunting pit, into which he fell and was trapped. As soon as he saw that the ass was secured, the lion ate the fox, saving the ass for later.

Similarly, those who betray their colleagues are often unknowingly destroyed along with their victims.

271

The Ass and the Frogs

An ass carrying a load of wood was crossing a bog one day. He slipped and fell. Not able to get up again, he began to groan and wail. The frogs in the bog, who heard all this moaning, said to him:

'What sort of a noise would you make if you had been living here for as long as we have? You, who have only fallen in for a moment!'

This fable could apply to an effeminate man who becomes impatient and complains about the slightest discomforts, while the rest of us put up with far worse things the whole time.

272

The Ass and the Mule Carrying the Same Heavy Loads

An ass and a mule were trudging along the road together. The ass noticed that their loads were the same and became indignant. He complained that the mule should carry more than him, for he judged him capable of carrying twice as much as himself. But, when they had gone a little further, the ass-driver noticed that the ass couldn't go on, and so he removed a part of his load and transferred it on to the mule. When they had gone a bit further, seeing that the ass was still exhausted, he took off a bit more of his load. Finally, removing the rest of it, he put it all on to the mule's back. Then the mule glanced over to his comrade and said to him:

'Well, my friend, don't you think it would be fair if I now got twice as much to eat?'

So it is with us: it is not just at the start but at the finish that we should judge each other's condition.

273

The Ass and the Gardener

An ass worked for a gardener. As he worked hard and didn't get much to eat, he begged Zeus to rescue him from the gardener and find him another master. Zeus answered his prayer and he was sold to a potter. But he again became discontented because he was loaded up even more and was made to carry clay and pottery. So he asked once more to change his master and was sold to a tanner. Thus, he fell into the hands of an even worse master. Upon seeing the sort of work his master did, he sighed to himself:

'Alas! How unlucky I am! I would have been better off staying with my previous masters; for this one, from what I can see, will tan my hide.'

This fable shows that servants should never regret their first masters until they have approved the next.

274

The Ass, the Raven
and the Wolf

An ass who had a sore on his back was grazing in a meadow. A raven landed, perched on the ass's back and started pecking at the sore. The ass, believing it was the sore that caused him such pain, began to bray and buck. The ass-driver, who saw this from some distance away, burst out laughing. A wolf who was passing by saw him and said to himself:

'How unfortunate we are! It's bad enough that when we are seen we are driven off, but when one of those comes near them they just laugh at it.'

This fable shows that mischievous people are recognized for what they are at first sight.

275

The Ass and the Lap-dog
or *The Dog and Its Master*

There was a man who owned a Maltese lap-dog and an ass. He was always playing with the dog. When he dined out, he would bring back titbits and throw them to the dog when it rushed up, wagging its tail. The ass was jealous of this and, one day, trotted up and started frisking around his master. But this resulted in the man getting a kick on the foot, and he grew very angry. So he drove the ass with a stick back to its manger, where he tied it up.

This fable shows that we are not all made to do the same things.

276

The Ass and the Dog
Travelling Together

An ass and a dog were taking the same route when they found a sealed document on the ground. The ass picked it up, broke the seal, opened it, read it aloud and the dog listened. It was all about fodder – that is to say hay, barley and straw. The dog became bored by this recital from the ass and said:

'Skip a few lines, friend. Maybe you'll come across something in there about meat and bones.'

The ass scanned the rest of the document and found nothing that was of interest to the dog, who then spoke up again:

'Throw the paper away. It's completely useless.'

277

The Ass and the Ass-driver

An ass who was being driven by an ass-driver strayed off the main path after a while and started to cross some steep slopes. When he fell over a precipice, the ass-driver, seizing the ass by the tail, tried to pull him back up. But, as the ass struggled frantically upside-down, the ass-driver let go and said:

'I give up. But you win the wrong victory.'

This fable applies to quarrelsome people.

278

The Ass and the Cicadas

Hearing some cicadas sing, an ass was charmed by their harmony and envied them their talent.

'What do you eat,' he asked them, 'that gives you such a beautiful song?'

'The dew,' they replied.

From then on, the ass waited for the dew and eventually starved to death.

So, when we long for things which are not in our nature, not only will we never be satisfied but we will bring upon ourselves even more misfortune.

279

The Ass Who Was Taken for a Lion

An ass, clothed in the skin of a lion, passed himself off in the eyes of everyone as a lion, and made everyone flee from him, both men and animals. But the wind came along and blew off the lion's skin, leaving him naked and exposed. Everyone then fell upon him when they saw this, and beat him with sticks and clubs.

Be poor and ordinary. Don't have pretensions to wealth or you will be exposed to ridicule and danger. For we cannot adapt ourselves to that which is alien to us.

280

The Ass Eating the Jerusalem Thorn, and the Fox

An ass was eating the prickly head of a Jerusalem Thorn. A fox saw him doing this and addressed him with these mocking words:

'I marvel that with such a loose and soft tongue you can chew so happily on something so hard.'

This fable addresses itself to those whose tongues utter hard and dangerous resolutions.

NOTE: The plant mentioned here, *paliourous* in Greek, is *Rhamnus paliurus*, commonly known as the Jerusalem Thorn or Christ's Thorn. It occurs throughout the Mediterranean region from Spain to Turkey. The moral of this fable suggests its use in opposing demagogues and fanatical orators in a political assembly.

281

The Ass Pretending to Be Lame, and the Wolf

An ass grazing in a small meadow saw a wolf creep up on him, so he pretended to be lame. The wolf, coming nearer, asked why he was limping. The ass replied that he had been jumping over a fence and had landed on a thorn. He advised the wolf to pull it out before eating him to avoid piercing his mouth. The wolf let himself be persuaded. While he was lifting up the ass's foot and concentrating on the hoof, the ass, with a sharp kick in the jaw, knocked his teeth out. In a bad way, the wolf said:

'I deserve what I got. For, having learned from my father the art of butchery, why should I want to try my hand at medicine?'

Thus, people who undertake things which are outside their abilities naturally bring themselves to disgrace.

282

The Bird-catcher and the Wild and Domesticated Pigeons

A bird-catcher spread his nets and tied his domesticated pigeons to them. Then he withdrew and watched from a distance what would happen. Some wild pigeons approached the captive birds and became entangled in the snares. The bird-catcher ran back and started to grab them. As he did so, they reproached the domesticated pigeons because, being of the same race, they should have warned them of the trap. But the domesticated pigeons replied:

'We are more concerned with preventing our master's displeasure than with pleasing our kindred.'

Thus it is with domestic slaves: you can't blame them when, for love of their masters, they fail to show love towards their own kind.

283

The Bird-catcher and the Crested Lark

A bird-catcher was setting up his snares. A crested lark, seeing him from afar, asked him what he was doing. He said that he was founding a city [*polis*]. Then he withdrew and hid himself. The lark, trusting in the man's words, flew down and was caught in a snare. The bird-catcher came running up and the lark said to him:

'Say, fellow! If this is the kind of city you are founding, it won't have many inhabitants!'

This fable shows that if houses and cities are deserted, it is usually because the leading men there are harsh and severe.

THE COMPLETE FABLES

284

The Bird-catcher and
the Stork

A bird-catcher, having laid some nets for cranes, watched his bait from a distance. Then a stork landed in the midst of the cranes and the bird-catcher ran back and caught her as well. She begged him to release her, saying that, far from harming men, she was very useful, for she ate snakes and other reptiles. The bird-catcher replied:

'If you really are harmless, then you deserve punishment anyway, for landing among the wicked.'

We, too, ought to flee from the company of wicked people so that no one takes us for the accomplice of their wrongdoings.

NOTE: Among the background of stork lore that the average ancient Greek would know in appreciating this fable, we might mention that in ancient Thessaly there was actually a law prohibiting the killing of storks because of their usefulness in destroying snakes.

285

The Bird-catcher and
the Partridge

A visitor turned up rather late at the house of a bird-catcher. Since the host had no food to offer him, he went to fetch his own partridge [used as a live decoy to lure wild birds] to have for supper. As he was on the point of killing her, she reproached him for his ingratitude:

'Have I not been most useful in calling the birds of my own tribe and delivering them up to you? And now you want to kill me?'

'All the more reason to sacrifice you,' the bird-catcher replied, 'since you have not even had mercy on your own kindred.'

This fable shows that those who betray their parents are odious not only to their victims, but also to those to whom they deliver them up.

286

The Hen and the Swallow

A hen found the eggs of a snake and carefully hatched them by sitting upon them and keeping them warm. A swallow, who had seen her doing this, said to her:

'What a fool you are! Why are you rearing these creatures who, once grown, will make you the first victim of their evildoing?'

Perversity cannot be tamed even by the kindest treatment.

287

The Hen That Laid the Golden Eggs

A man had a beautiful hen who laid golden eggs. Believing that she might have a lump of gold in her belly, the man killed her and found that she was just the same inside as other hens. He had hoped to find riches in one go, and was thus deprived of even the little profit that he had.

This fable shows that we should be content with our lot, and shun insatiable greed.

288

The Tail and the Rest of the Body of the Snake

One day, the snake's tail developed pretensions to be the leader and led the advance. The remaining parts of the body of the snake said to it:

'How can you lead us when you have no eyes or nose like other animals?'

But they could not persuade the tail, and ultimately common sense was defeated. The tail led the way, pulling blindly on the rest of the body so that in the end the snake fell into a hole full of stones and bruised her backbone and her whole body. Then the tail addressed the head, fawning and beseeching:

'Save us, please, mistress, for I was in the wrong to enter into a quarrel with you.'

This fable confounds crafty and perverse men who rebel against their masters.

NOTE: A literal translation of the title of this fable would be 'The Tail and the Limbs of the Snake', since the Greeks extended the concept of 'limbs' beyond arms and legs to include bodily frame, but in English this does not make sense.

289

The Snake, the House-ferret
and the Mice

A snake and a house-ferret were fighting each other in a certain house where they lived. The mice of the house, who were forever being eaten by one or the other of them, came quietly out of their holes when they heard them fighting. At the sight of the mice, the two combatants gave up their battle and turned on the mice.

It is the same in the city-states [poleōn]; people who interfere in the quarrels of the demagogues become, without suspecting it, the victims of both sides.

290

The Snake and the Crab

A snake and a crab frequented the same place. The crab continually behaved towards the snake in all simplicity and kindness. But the snake was always cunning and perverse. The crab ceaselessly urged the snake to behave towards him with honesty and to imitate his own manner towards him; he did not listen. So, indignant, the crab waited for an occasion when the snake was asleep, grabbed it and killed it. Seeing it stretched out dead, the crab called out:

'Hey, friend! It's no use being straight now that you are dead, you should have done that when I was urging you to before; then you wouldn't have had to be put to death!'

One could rightly tell this fable with regard to people who, during their life, are wicked towards their friends and do them a service after their death.

291

The Trodden-on Snake
and Zeus

The snake, heavily trodden on so often by men's feet, went to Zeus to complain. Zeus said to it:

'If you had bitten the first one who trod on you, the second one would not have tried to do so.'

This fable shows that those who hold their own against the first people who attack them make themselves formidable to others who do so.

292

The Child Who Ate the
Sacrificial Viscera

Some shepherds sacrificed a goat in the countryside and invited their neighbours. Among these was a poor woman who brought her child with her. As the feast progressed, the child, whose stomach was distended with too much food, felt ill and cried:

'Mother, I'm bringing up my guts!'

'Not yours,' she replied, 'but those you have eaten.'

This fable is addressed to the debtor who is always ready to take the assets of others, then when one claims them back he is aggrieved as much as if he were paying with his own money.

NOTE: This fable is actually a coarse peasant joke, perhaps even based on an amusing true incident with a child. When an animal was sacrificed to the gods, it was customary for the subsequent feast to commence with all the guests present eating the viscera – namely, the heart, lungs, liver and kidneys. These choice morsels were a solemn delicacy at a sacrifice. In this story the child vomits up guts, thinking they are his own, whereas they are the goat's.

293

The Child Catching Locusts, and the Scorpion

A child was catching locusts in front of the city wall. After having caught a certain number of them, he saw a scorpion. He took it for a locust and, cupping his hand, was about to put it in his palm when the scorpion, rearing his spike, said to the child:

'Would that you had done that! For then you would have lost the locusts that you have already caught!'

This fable shows us that we should not behave in the same way towards good and wicked people.

294

The Child and the Raven

A woman consulted the diviners about her infant son. They predicted that he would be killed by a raven [*korax*]. Terror-stricken by this prediction, she had a huge chest constructed and shut the boy up inside it to prevent him from being killed by a raven. And every day, at a given time, she opened it and gave the child as much food as he needed. Then, one day when she had opened the chest and was putting back the lid, the child foolishly stuck his head out. So it happened that the *korax* [hooked handle] on the chest fell down on to the top of his head and killed him.

NOTE: This fable depends upon a pun, the same Greek word, *korax*, meaning both 'raven' and 'hooked handle, like a raven's beak'. Every Athenian would also be familiar with the idea of a boy being shut up in a box, as it was a mythological motif.

295

The Son and the Painted Lion

There was a timid old man who was afraid of his only son's passion for hunting, for the son was full of courage. In a dream he saw that his son would be killed by a lion. Dreading that this dream would come true, the father built a dwelling for his son of great magnificence, set in a high place where he could keep his eye on him. In order to distract and please him, he had commissioned for his chamber paintings of every kind of animal, and among these was a lion. But looking at all these did not distract the young man from his boredom.

One day, he approached the painting and cursed the lion in it:

'You damned beast, it's because of you and my father's lying dream that I am cooped up here in this prison for women. What can I do to you?'

And, as he said this, he struck his fist against the wall to blind the lion. But a splinter got lodged under his fingernail and he could not get it out. This became greatly inflamed, brought on a fever and swelled up to an enormous size. The fever raged so fiercely that the young man died of it.

The lion, even though it was only a painted one, had indeed killed the young man, just as his father had foreseen.

This shows that we should bravely face the fate which awaits us, rather than try to outwit or trick Fate, for what is destined cannot be evaded.

296

The Child Thief and His Mother

A child stole the writing-tablet [*delton*] of his fellow pupil at school and brought it home to his mother. Instead of chastising him, she praised him. And another time he stole a cloak [*himation*] and gave it to her and she praised him even more. Later, coming of age and becoming a young man, he brought her ever more important stolen goods. But, one day, he was caught in the act. His hands were tied behind his back and he was led off to the executioner. His mother went with him and beat her chest. He declared that he would like to whisper something in her ear. As soon as she bent to listen, he grabbed her ear lobe and severed it with one bite of his teeth. She reproached him for his impiety: not content with the crimes he had already committed, he went on to mutilate his mother! He replied:

'If, from the time I brought you the first writing-tablet that I stole, you had thrashed me, I would not have come to this pass where I am now: I would not be being led to my death.'

This fable shows that those who are not reprimanded from the outset grow up and get worse.

NOTE: Liddell and Scott, in their *Lexicon*, maintained that the Greeks called a writing-tablet a *deltos* because writing-tablets had once been shaped like deltas. But there were never any delta-shaped writing-tablets, and this strange suggestion has been dropped in the 1996 edition, where the cognate *daltos* in the Cyprian dialect is noted but no etymology is given otherwise. We should therefore point out that *deltos* comes from the Ugaritic *daltu*, which survives also in Hebrew as *daleth*.

297

The Child Bather

One day, a child bathing in a river was in danger of drowning. Seeing a traveller pass by, he called out to him for help. The traveller scolded him for his recklessness. The boy cried out:

'But get me out of trouble first! Later, when you have saved me, make your reproaches!'

This fable applies to people who give others a pretext for treating them unkindly.

298

The Receiver of a Deposit of Money, and the God Horkos

A man, to whom a friend had entrusted a deposit of money, was intending to withhold repayment. When this friend issued a court summons for him to take an oath [*horkos*], he became anxious and departed for the countryside. At the town gates he met a lame man, also leaving, and he asked him who he was and where he was going. The latter replied that he was the god Horkos [Oath] and that he was seeking out the ungodly. So the man asked a second question:

'And after how long an interval is it that you usually return to the towns?'

'After forty, sometimes thirty, years,' he replied.

After that, the man didn't hesitate to swear the next day that he had never received the money. But he came face to face with Horkos, who led him off to hurl him from a cliff. The man moaned:

'You told me that you didn't come back for thirty years, but you haven't even granted me a single day in safety.'

Horkos replied:

'You ought to know that when someone wishes to provoke me, I have the habit of returning on the same day.'

This fable shows that there is no specified day for divine punishment of the godless.

299

The Father and His Daughters

A man who had two daughters gave one in marriage to a gardener, the other to a potter. After a while he paid a visit to the gardener's wife and asked her how she was getting on and how their business was. She replied that things were to her liking and that she had only one thing to ask of the gods: a storm and rain to water the vegetables. A little later he went to visit the potter's wife at home and asked her how she was getting on. She replied that they lacked nothing and that she had but one wish to make: that the weather should stay fine and the sun shine to dry the pots.

'If you want good weather and your sister wants bad weather, with which of you should I join my prayers?'

Likewise, if one has two opposite ventures at the same time, one naturally wants success for both of them.

300

The Partridge and the Man

A man caught a partridge while hunting and was about to kill it. She pleaded with him:

'Let me live! In my place I would bring you lots of partridges.'

'All the more reason to kill you,' replied the man, 'since you wish to ensnare your friends and comrades.'

This shows that the man who weaves a plot against his friends will himself fall into danger and ambushes.

NOTE: It was the custom in ancient Greece to trap partridges by luring them to land among snares by placing a tame partridge on the ground.

301

The Thirsty Pigeon

A pigeon, driven by thirst, saw a basin [*krater*] of water in a painting and believed it to be real. So, with a great flapping of wings, she hurled herself against it rashly and broke the tips of her wings. Falling to the ground, she was caught by a passer-by who was there.

Similarly, some men carried away by the strength of their passions thoughtlessly undertake ventures and hurry, without hesitation, to their ruin.

NOTE: The Greek terminology for the different pigeons and doves is muddled. *Peristera*, which is used here, generally refers to the domestic pigeon. But, in this instance, the pigeon was clearly a wild bird. In the next fable, however, a domesticated pigeon is referred to.

302

The Pigeon and the Crow

A pigeon, kept in a dovecote, boasted loudly of her fertility. Hearing this, a crow said to her:

'Hey, friend! Stop boasting like that. For the more children you have, the more you should lament slavery.'

It is the same with domestic slaves. The worst off are the ones who have children in slavery.

303

The Two Carrying-pouches

Once upon a time, when Prometheus created men, he hung from them two carrying-pouches. One of these contained the deficiencies of other people and was hung in front. The other contained our own faults, which he suspended behind us. The result of this was that men could see directly down into the pouch containing other people's failings, but were unable to see their own.

One can apply this fable to the muddle-headed person who, blind to his own faults, meddles with those of others which do not concern him at all.

NOTE: *Perai* were leather wallets or carrying-pouches slung over the shoulders and frequently used in ancient Greece for carrying victuals. They are often mentioned by Homer in the *Odyssey*. The image of the two carrying-pouches entered profoundly into classical culture; we find Catullus, the Roman poet, saying (22.21): 'Everybody has his own delusion assigned to him: but we do not see that part of the bag which hangs on our back.'

304

The Monkey and the Fishermen

A monkey perching in a lofty tree saw some fishermen casting their drag-net into a river and watched what they did. Later, leaving their net, they withdrew a short distance to have their lunch. Then the monkey, climbing down from the tree, tried to do what they did, for this animal, it is said, has a natural aptitude for mimicry. But, as soon as he touched the net, he got caught up in it and was in danger of drowning. He then said:

'I only got what I deserve; why have I taken up fishing without having learned how to first?'

This fable shows that by meddling in affairs which one doesn't understand, not only does one gain nothing, but one also does oneself harm.

305

The Monkey and the Dolphin

It is the custom when voyaging by sea to take with one some little Maltese terriers and some monkeys to amuse oneself with during the crossing. So, then, a man who was sailing the seas had a monkey with him. When they were off Cape Sounion of Attica [a promontory near Athens], a violent storm broke, the vessel capsized and everyone jumped overboard to save themselves, including the monkey. A dolphin saw him and, taking him for a man, slid underneath him, held him up and carried him towards dry land. When they arrived at the maritime port of Piraeus he asked the monkey if he was an Athenian. The monkey replied that he was and that he even had illustrious Athenian parents. The dolphin asked him if he also knew Piraeus. The monkey, believing him to be speaking of a man, said yes, and that in fact he was one of his best friends. Enraged by such a lie, the dolphin dived down into the water and the monkey was drowned.

This fable shows that men who do not know the truth delude other people.

306

The Monkey and the Camel

At an assembly of the beasts, a monkey got up and danced. He was enthusiastically applauded by everyone present. A jealous camel wanted to earn the same praise. He got up and also tried to dance, but he did such absurd things that the other animals became disgusted and beat him out of their sight with sticks.

This fable is suitable for those people who, through envy, compete with those who are their betters.

307

The Monkey's Children

The monkeys, it is said, give birth to two children at once. Of these two children the mother cherishes and feeds one with tender care, whereas she despises and neglects the other one. So it happens that, by divine fate, the little one that the mother takes care of with love and clasps in her arms is suffocated to death by her, and the one she neglects reaches a perfect maturity.

This fable shows that chance is more powerful than forethought.

308

The Sea Voyagers

Some people boarded a ship and took to sea. When they were out in the open, a violent storm blew up and the vessel was in danger of sinking. One by one the passengers tore at their clothes, invoking the gods of their countries with tears and moans and promising to make offerings of thanks if they escaped and the boat was saved. But the tempest stopped and calm was restored. So they began to make merry, to dance, to leap about like people do who have escaped from an unforeseen danger. Then the stout-spirited steersman sprang up and said to them:

'My friends, let us rejoice, but let us do so like people who may yet again encounter the storm.'

The fable shows that you shouldn't become too elated with success, and that you should remember the fickleness of chance.

309

The Rich Man and the Tanner

A rich man came to live next door to a tanner. As he couldn't bear the bad smell from the tanner's yard, he kept on urging him to move somewhere else. The tanner continually postponed the move, promising to go in a little while. But, as their dispute was ceaselessly prolonged, the rich man eventually got used to the smell and stopped pestering the tanner.

This fable shows that habit ameliorates the sources of annoyance.

310

The Rich Man and
the Mourners

A wealthy man had two daughters. One of them died and so he hired some mourners. The remaining daughter said to her mother:

'We are so wretched, for although we are the bereaved ones, we do not know how to make the lamentations. Whereas these women, who are nothing to us, beat themselves and weep with so much violence.'

The mother replied:

'Don't be surprised, my child, if these women make such pitiable lamentations; they do it for money.'

Thus it is that some people, prompted by their own interest, do not hesitate to trade in the unhappiness of others.

311

The Shepherd and the Sea

A shepherd who pastured a flock of sheep by the sea, seeing how calm the waves were, conceived a desire to sail forth and do some trading. So he sold his sheep, bought some dates and set sail. But a heavy storm arose and the boat was in danger of sinking. So he threw his cargo overboard and, with great difficulty, saved himself with his empty boat. Some time later a man came along. As he was admiring the calmness of the sea, which seemed quiet at the moment, our shepherd spoke up and said to him:

'Ah, my good man, she wants some more dates, it seems. That's why she appears calm.'

This fable shows that mishaps serve as lessons to men.

312

The Shepherd and the Dog
Who Fawned upon Sheep

A shepherd had a huge dog and he used to throw it the stillborn lambs and dying sheep to eat. Then, one day when the flock was resting in the fold, he saw his dog approach some ewes and fawn upon them.

'Hey, you!' he called out to it, 'may the fate you wish on them befall you instead!'

This fable is addressed to flatterers.

313

The Shepherd and
the Wolf Cubs

A shepherd found some wolf cubs and reared them with great care in the hope that, when grown, they would not only guard his own sheep but would also seize the sheep of other people and bring them to him. But, as soon as they reached maturity, they took an opportunity when they had nothing to fear and began to ravage his flock. When he realized this calamity he groaned and said:

'It serves me right. For why did I rescue the young of animals which one has to destroy when they are grown up?'

In saving bad people we unwittingly give them the power to turn against us first of all.

314

The Shepherd and the Wolf
Raised with the Dogs

A shepherd found a new-born wolf cub and took it home to rear with his dogs. When the wolf cub grew to maturity, if a wolf sometimes carried off a sheep he would chase it, along with the dogs. When, occasionally, the dogs couldn't catch up with the wolf and in consequence turned back, he pursued it until he caught up with it, and would then have his share of the spoils like the wolf he was. Then he would turn back. If a wolf didn't kill a sheep outside the sheepfold, he would kill one himself on the sly and eat it with the dogs. But, finally, the shepherd guessed this and understood what was happening, so he killed the wolf and hung him from a tree.

This fable shows that the naturally wicked cannot be given a good character.

315

The Shepherd and
the Wolf Cub

A shepherd found a tiny wolf and reared it. Then, when it was a cub, he taught it to steal the sheep from the neighbouring flocks. One day, the wolf confronted him and said:

'Now that you have got me into the habit of stealing, take care you don't miss any of your own sheep.'

People who are naturally clever, once trained to pillage and theft, as often as not do more harm to their masters than to strangers.

316

The Shepherd and the Sheep

A shepherd drove his sheep into an oak wood where he spotted a huge oak tree covered in acorns. He spread out his cloak beneath the tree, then climbed up it and shook the acorns down. The sheep, eating the acorns, also ate the cloak accidentally. When the shepherd climbed down and saw the damage, he cried out:

'Wicked creatures! You provide wool for others to clothe themselves, but for me, the one who feeds you, all you do is deprive me of my cloak!'

Thus, plenty of people stupidly oblige those who are nothing to them, and behave shabbily to their next of kin.

NOTE: The practice of using acorns for both human and animal food has been common among country people throughout history. There is even a special term in English for the use of acorns as animal fodder: pannage. In Saxon times laws were passed allowing peasants the right of pannage for their swine. Acorns can be used as food for humans, though the flavour is improved if they are dried. Dried acorns can also provide a nourishing flour. In America the sweet acorns of the bur oak were popular with the Chippewa Indians, who roasted and boiled them and especially liked to put them into duck broth. The British Board of Agriculture issued a pamphlet in the 1920s urging the use of acorns for animal fodder. Also in the 1920s the British medical journal, the *Lancet*, published an analysis of the constituents of acorns: 5.2 per cent protein, 43 per cent fat, 45 per cent carbohydrates as starch, 6.3 per cent water. (The remaining ·5 per cent was presumably bitter principles.)

317

The Shepherd Who Let a Wolf into the Fold, and the Dog

A shepherd, herding his sheep into the fold, also shut a wolf up with them. His dog, who realized that this should not happen, said to him:

'How can you, whose livelihood is sheep, let a wolf go in with them?'

The company of the wicked in itself causes most harm, and even death.

318

The Joking Shepherd

A shepherd who led his flock rather far from the village frequently indulged in the following practical joke. He called to the people of the village to help him, crying that wolves were attacking his sheep. Two or three times the villagers were alarmed and rushed forth, then returned home having been fooled. But, in the end, it happened that some wolves really did appear. While they ravaged the flock, the shepherd called out for help to the villagers. But they, imagining that he was hoaxing them as usual, didn't bother with him. So it was that he lost his sheep.

This fable shows that liars gain only one thing, which is not to be believed even when they tell the truth.

319

Polemos and Hybris

All the gods, having decided to get married, each took the wife that fate assigned to him. The God of War [Polemos], being left for the last drawing of lots, could find only Wanton Violence [Hybris]. He fell madly in love with her and married her. That is why he goes everywhere where she goes.

Everywhere where wanton violence appears in a city or among the nations, war and battle go also.

NOTE: In this fable, as in most others, the Olympian deities of the official state religions are ignored and more basic or popular gods are referred to. The Greek word *polemos* means 'war', and Polemos is thus the personification of war. The official god of war, Ares – known in Latin as Mars – is ignored here altogether.

320

The River and the Hide

A river, seeing an oxhide floating in her waters, asked it its name.
  'I am called Hard,' it replied.
  Then, increasing the effect of her current upon it, the river replied:
  'Find another name, for I shall quickly make you soft.'

Often, bold and arrogant people are overwhelmed by the misfortunes of life.

321

The Sheared Sheep

A sheep who had been clumsily sheared said to the person who had done it:

'If it's my wool you want, then cut higher up. If you want my meat, then just kill me and get it over with. But don't keep torturing me like this.'

This fable applies to those who are clumsy in their craft.

322

Prometheus and Men

On the orders of Zeus, Prometheus made men and beasts. But Zeus remarked that there were many more animals than men and instructed him to transform some of the beasts into men. Prometheus carried out this order. It resulted in those who hadn't been given human form in the beginning taking the shape of men but having the souls of beasts.

This fable applies to clumsy and savage men.

NOTE: The other early recorded reference in Greek literature to Prometheus as a creator of men is by the comic poet Philemon, fourth century BC. But the history and evolution of the figure of Prometheus is a subject too vast for us to consider here.

323

The Rose and the Amaranth

An amaranth, which grew beside a rose, said to it:

'How beautiful you are! You are the delight of gods and men. I congratulate you on your beauty and your scent!'

The rose replied:

'I only live but for a few days, Amaranth. And even if no one cuts me I wither. But you, you are always in flower and you remain ever young.'

It would be better to remain content with little than to live in luxury for a short time, and then to exchange it for misfortune and even death.

NOTE: The amaranth, *amarantos*, was a never-fading flower. *Marantikos* means 'wasting away' or 'withered'. *Maransis* means 'decay' or 'causing to die away'. Since in Greek the addition of the letter 'a' to an adjective means 'not-' or 'non-', the word was used to mean 'unfading, undecaying'. But what actual plant was intended? In ancient Greece the amaranth was sacred to the goddess Artemis of Ephesus and, as a symbol of immortality, was used to decorate tombs. But the tradition of the amaranth goes back into remotest Indo-European tradition, long before the Greeks existed as a people.

In Sanskrit the word *amara* means also 'undying, immortal, imperishable' and in the Indian epic, the *Mahābhārata*, Amara actually appears as a deity. The number 33 and the letter 'u' were also called *amara* for mystical reasons. The word was also applied to the umbilical cord, to the afterbirth, to quicksilver, to a sacred mountain and was the name of the residence of the god Indra. But the Hindus, too, had a tradition of an imperishable flower, and they called several plants by the name of *amara*, including even a species of pine. There were at least half a dozen different Indian amaranths, in fact, some associated with the god Amara and some merely using the word as a descriptive adjective. No modern scholar seems to have sorted it all out. But the importance of the tradition cannot be overestimated.

Amaratva (immortality) was 'the condition of the gods'. So, in effect, the amaranths of the Hindus were actually the gods themselves. The only major

Greek divinity to whom the name amaranth was applied was Artemis, whose origins were in Asia Minor. Roscher points out in his *Mythological Lexicon* that amaranth in Greece sometimes became Amarynthos, and that he was the father of Narcissus. And he refers to the geographer Strabo, who mentions in his *Geography* (X, 9, 448) an archaic Temple of Artemis Amarynthia on the island of Euboea. Strabo also mentions a site called Amarynthia at Eretria in Euboea, which was probably a very early sacred precinct. These archaic Euboean occurrences are significant in that they are evidently survivals of pre-Greek traditions. Burkert has pointed out the significance of Euboea as a link between Greece and the East in early times (*The Orientalizing Revolution: Near-Eastern Influence on Greek Culture in the Early Archaic Age* by Walter Burkert, Harvard University Press, 1995, p. 10), referring to Euboea as a 'relatively affluent community in the tenth and ninth centuries [BC] which was open to trade with the East', where ancient traditions, both Indo-European and Semitic, took root.

S. A. Handford was wrong to imply in the earlier Penguin Aesop (note to Fable 142) that the amaranth tradition was a late one, whereas, on the contrary, it was so ancient that we cannot trace its origins since they go back further than any texts. Nor was he correct to say that the word was late, since, in the form amaranth, it is earlier than Greek civilization itself at Euboea and, as we have seen, it goes back to proto-Indo-European since it survives in Sanskrit and must therefore originate before the Aryans migrated to India and separated from the peoples who later became the Greeks. The concept of the amaranth cannot, therefore, be more recent than 2000 BC, and is probably much earlier. In all probability the imperishable flower as symbol of the immortal gods goes back tens of thousands of years; we know that Neanderthal men threw flowers into graves, and the proximity to nature of early mankind makes such associations obvious.

As for the actual plant referred to in the fable, it may have been the weed ingloriously known in English as the pigweed. A more fashionable 'amaranth' cultivated by gardeners today is 'love-lies-bleeding'. But amaranth was never a term of botanical precision and the father of botany, Theophrastus, appears not to mention it (it is not in his *Historia Plantarum* but, as there is no index to his *De Causis Plantarum*, we cannot be certain for that work), evidently not considering it a precise enough term to describe any single plant. In short, the amaranth, with its associations with immortality, was more an idea than a plant and, from early times, any plant which dried well or had imperishable aspects partook of the idea of amaranth in the sense of the Sanskrit *amaratva* – the condition of the gods who never die.

324

The Pomegranate Tree, the Apple Tree, the Olive Tree and the Bramble Bush

One day the pomegranate tree, the apple tree and the olive tree were contesting the quality of their fruits. The discussion became rather animated and a bramble, who was listening to them from a nearby hedgerow, said:

'Dear friends, do let us stop quarrelling with one another!'

It is thus that, at those times when the best of the citizens are divided, people of low birth try to assume importance.

NOTE: In our more egalitarian times the nature of this joke may be rather lost on us, but its point was to astonish and amuse by the fact that the despised bramble could presume to consider itself a 'friend' of the stately fruit trees, as if a slave were to go up to a master and invite him to sit down.

325

The Trumpeter

A trumpeter who summoned the assembly of troops was captured by the enemy and called out:

'Do not kill me, comrades, without due consideration and for no reason. For I have not killed any of you and apart from my brass [*chalkos*] I have nothing.'

But someone replied:

'All the more reason for you to die, since, not being able to go to war yourself, you arouse everyone else to combat.'

This fable shows that those who provoke evil are the more guilty.

NOTE: In Greek the same word, *chalkos*, means copper, brass or bronze, but in this instance clearly it is used in the colloquial sense of 'a brass'. As for the ancient Greek trumpet, *salpinx*, it was specifically a war trumpet.

326

The Mole and His Mother

A mole – the mole is a blind creature – said to his mother that he could see. To put him to the test, his mother gave him a grain of frankincense [*libanōtos*] and asked him what it was.

'It's a pebble,' he said.

'My child,' replied the mother, 'not only are you bereft of sight, but you have also lost your sense of smell.'

Similarly, boastful people promise the impossible and are proved powerless in the most simple affairs.

327

The Wild Boar and the Fox

A wild boar was sharpening his tusks on a tree trunk one day. A fox asked him why he did this when there was neither huntsman nor danger threatening him.

'I do so for a good reason,' he replied. 'For if I am suddenly surprised by danger I wouldn't have the time to sharpen my tusks. But now I will find them ready to do their duty.'

This fable shows that it is no good waiting until danger comes to be ready.

328

The Wild Boar, the Horse and the Huntsman

The wild boar and the horse shared the same pasture. Because the wild boar continually ruined the grass and muddied the water, the horse, wanting to have his revenge, turned to a hunter for help. But the latter announced that he couldn't lend him a hand unless he would agree to wear a bridle and to carry him on his back. The horse yielded to all his demands. Then the huntsman mounted on to his back, took and overcame the boar and, leading the horse home, he tied him to the stable rack.

Thus, blind rage makes many people wreak vengeance on their enemies, thereby throwing themselves under the yoke of other people's power.

329

The Sow and the Dog Insulting One Another

The sow and the dog were outdoing each other with insults. The sow swore by Aphrodite that she would tear the dog to pieces. The dog replied ironically:

'It's all very well for you to swear by Aphrodite. It's evident she loves you with all her tenderness, she who absolutely refuses to admit to her temple anyone who has tasted of your impure flesh.'

'That is even more proof that the goddess cherishes me, since it means that she simply throws out anyone who kills me or maltreats me in any way at all. As for you, you smell bad – worse when you're alive than when you're dead.'

This fable shows that prudent rhetors skilfully turn the insults of their enemies into commendation.

330

The Wasps, the Partridges and the Ploughman

Some wasps and some partridges, desperate with thirst, went to a ploughman to ask him for a drink, promising in exchange for a little water to render him a service. The partridges offered to dig his vines and the wasps offered to buzz around to divert thieves with their stings. The farmer replied:

'But I have two oxen who do everything for me without any promises. It would be better that I give them water rather than you.'

This fable applies to corrupt men who promise their services and cause great damage.

331

The Wasp and the Snake

One day, a wasp settled on the head of a snake and tormented it, stinging him without respite. The snake, mad with pain, not being able to take revenge on his enemy, put his head under the wheel of a wagon. And thus the wasp died with him.

This fable shows that some people do not recoil from the idea of dying with their enemies.

332

The Bull and the Wild Goats

A bull was being chased by a lion and took refuge in a cave where there were some wild goats. Gored and butted by them, he said:

'If I endure your blows it's not because I am afraid of you. What I am in fear of is standing outside the cave.'

It is often thus, that the fear of someone stronger than us makes us tolerate the attacks of someone weaker than ourselves.

333

The Peacock and the Crane

The peacock was making fun of the crane and criticizing his colour:

'I am dressed in gold and purple,' he said. 'You wear nothing beautiful on your wings.'

'But I,' replied the crane, 'sing near to the stars and I mount up to the heights of heaven. You, like the cockerels, can only mount the hens down below.'

It would be better to be renowned and in poor garments than to live without honour in rich attire.

334

The Peacock and the Jackdaw

The birds were consulting together on the choice of a king. The peacock demanded to be named king by virtue of his beauty. And the birds were about to vote for him when the jackdaw called out:

'But if you reign, what help can we expect from you when the eagle comes hunting for us?'

This fable shows that you should not reprimand those who, foreseeing future dangers, take precautions in advance.

335

The Cicada and the Fox

A cicada was singing at the top of a lofty tree. A fox, who wanted to eat it, thought up the following trick. He took up his position opposite her, he admired her delightful singing and he invited her to come down. He said he would like to see the creature which possessed such a beautiful voice. Suspecting the trap, the cicada tore off a leaf and let it fall. The fox pounced upon it, believing it was the cicada.

'You are mistaken, friend,' she said to him, 'if you believed that I would come down. I have mistrusted foxes ever since the day when I saw the wings of a cicada in a fox's droppings.'

The misfortunes of a neighbour make a sensible man wiser.

336

The Cicada and the Ants

It was winter. Their grain was damp and the ants were drying it. A cicada, who was hungry, asked them for something to eat. The ants replied:

'Why didn't you too store up some provisions during the summer?'

'I didn't have the time for that,' replied the cicada. 'I was singing melodiously.'

The ants made fun of her:

'Ah well,' they said, 'since you sang in summer you can dance in winter.'

This fable shows that in all things one should beware of negligence, if one wishes to avoid danger and trouble.

NOTE: Some people have made rude remarks about the cicada's sound being unpleasant. However, it is a most striking and fascinating phenomenon. Cicadas generally sing in groups, and the most remarkable aspect of their song is that it comes in collective waves, so that it is rather like listening to the sea landing on the shore. Many find the orchestral music of the cicadas a comforting solace, especially if they are lonely. No one can be truly alone as long as the cicadas are singing. In China, cicadas are sold in little bamboo cages, taken home and hung in the house for their pleasant song, carefully fed and treated as pets. Sometimes the Chinese carry their cicadas along with them as company, enjoying their loud song in the way that many people carry small radios.

337

The Wall of the House
and the Stake

A house wall, brutally pierced by a stake, cried:
'Why are you piercing me, who have done you no harm?'
The stake replied:
'It's not me who is the cause of your suffering but the one who is violently hitting me from behind.'

NOTE: There is no moral attached to this fable. The fable itself is peculiar in that it uses the word *palos* for 'stake' (which became *palus* in Latin and 'pale' in obsolete English usage). According to Liddell and Scott, this meaning for *palos* is a Byzantine usage, as the traditional meaning of *palos* was a 'lot' which was drawn. Can this be a very late fable? Or do we have here early evidence of a folk usage of *palos* which did not find its way into formal texts until centuries later? In the 1996 edition of Liddell and Scott, the reference 'Aesop. 402' has been inserted, referring to this fable. Otherwise no use of the word to mean 'stake' is recorded before the second century AD. The word *toichos* is also not the usual word for 'wall', but was used specifically for house walls; its use, however, goes back to Homer.

338

The Archer and the Lion

A very skilful archer went up the mountain to go hunting there. All the animals fled from him except for the lion, which alone challenged him to fight. The archer let fly an arrow which struck him. Then he said:

'Such is my messenger, after which I shall come for you myself.'

The injured lion took flight. A fox then called out to the lion to have courage and not to run away. But the lion replied:

'You can't fool me. If he has such a stinging messenger, were he to come for me himself what should I do?'

One should consider the end at the outset and consequently secure one's safety.

339

The Billy-Goat and the Vine

Just at the time when the vine bursts with young shoots, a billy-goat nibbled the buds. The vine said to him:

'Why do you damage me like this? Is there no more green grass? You needn't think I'll provide any less wine than is needed when they come to sacrifice you.'

This fable confounds people who are ungrateful and who would like to steal from their friends.

340

The Hyenas

They say that hyenas change their sex each year and become males and females alternately. Now, one day a male hyena attempted an unnatural sex act with a female hyena. The female responded:

'If you do that, friend, remember that what you do to me will soon be done to you.'

This is what one could say to the judge [archon] *concerning his successor, if he had to suffer some indignity from him.*

NOTE: This fable appears to have Athenian origins, since the *archons* were specifically Athenian judges, or chief magistrates, nine in number.

As for the hyenas, this was also a subject for discussion at Athens in the fourth century BC. At that time Aristotle was writing his accounts of the sexuality of hyenas which appear in his works *History of Animals* and *On the Generation of Animals* (trans. A. L. Peck, 1942, Loeb Library Vol. 366), and in both cases he felt that he had to rebut current gossip on the subject. In the former (VI, xxxii, 579b16) he writes: 'They say that the hyena has both male and female sexual organs. But this is not true.' He then goes on to describe the minute anatomical details, according to his usual practice. In the latter work (III, vi, 757a2) he writes of the 'silly' story which says that hyenas have both male and female sexual organs. He also cites an earlier author, Herodorus of Heraclea, who flourished circa 400 BC, as writing in a book, probably his *History of Herakles*, that the hyena mounts and is mounted in alternate years. Aristotle then goes on to explain how this erroneous interpretation arose from a too casual inspection of the admittedly confusing genitalia of hyenas.

The importance of all this is that through his zoological concerns Aristotle is led to give us what is probably the precise origin of our fable, together with its approximate earliest possible date. The notion that hyenas mount and are mounted in alternate years is specifically suggested by Herodorus, and it is probable that he is the source of the anecdote which led directly to this fable being written.

341

The Hyena and the Fox

They say that hyenas change their sex every year and become alternately male and female. Now, a girl hyena, fancying a fox, reproached him bitterly for rejecting her advances and driving her away from him when she had wished to become friendly with him.

'It's not to me you should complain,' retorted the fox, 'but to your own nature, which gives me no way of knowing whether you would be my girlfriend or my boyfriend.'

This relates to the sexually ambiguous man.

NOTE: As with Fable 340, this fable is based upon the notion that hyenas change sex every year, as reported by Herodorus and dismissed by Aristotle. See the note to Fable 340.

342

The Sow and the Bitch, on the Ease of Bearing Offspring

A sow and a bitch were arguing about their ease of bearing offspring. The bitch claimed that of all quadrupeds she was by far the quickest to give birth.

'When you say that,' retorted the sow, 'remember that you only give birth to blind puppies.'

This fable shows that things should be judged not by their rapidity but by the care with which they are performed.

343

The Bald Horseman

A bald man who had put false hair on the top of his head was riding along the road. A puff of wind blew off the man's false hair and the people who saw it all burst out laughing at his misfortune. So, stopping his horse, the man said:

'Is it so strange that I can't keep hair which isn't my own on my head when it couldn't even stay on the head of its rightful owner where it grew naturally?'

It is no good our grieving from accidents which arise. What Nature did not give us at birth we know we can never keep. Naked we come, naked we depart.

344

The Miser

A miser turned his riches into gold, made an ingot of it and buried it in a certain place where he might be said also to have deposited his heart and spirit. Every day he went to gloat over his treasure. A labourer watched him and guessed what he was up to and, digging up the ingot, carried it off. Some time later the miser returned to the spot and found the empty hole. He began to moan and tear out his hair. A passer-by, seeing him lamenting thus and learning the reason why, said to him:

'Don't despair like that, friend. For when you had all that gold you didn't really have it. Take a stone and put that in the earth instead, and imagine that it is your gold. It will serve the same purpose. For, as far as I can see, even when the gold was there you made no use of it.'

This fable shows that, without enjoyment, possession is nothing.

345

The Blacksmith and His Puppy

A blacksmith had a puppy. While he was forging the puppy slept, but when he sat down to eat the puppy went and sat down beside him. Throwing him a bone, the blacksmith said to the puppy:

'Wretched creature! Always sleeping! When I strike my anvil you sleep but as soon as I move my jaws you wake up instantly!'

Sleepy and idle people who live off the labour of others will recognize themselves in this fable.

346

Winter and Spring

One day, Winter mocked Spring and made fun of her: as soon as Spring arrived, no one had any peace any longer. Some people would go off to the meadows or to the forests, happy to gather blossom, lilies and roses, admire them and put them in their hair. Others would take to their ships and perhaps cross the sea to meet men of other lands. No one had any further fear of winds or floods.

'I am like a ruler and absolute despot,' said Winter. 'I bid them to turn their gaze not up to the heavens but to cast their eyes down to the earth in fear and trembling, and to stay in sometimes and resign themselves to protecting their homes all day long.'

'That's why,' replied the Spring, 'people have pleasure in being rid of you. But, on the contrary, my very name to them is a thing of beauty, the most beautiful of all names, by Zeus! So that when I disappear they treasure my memory and as soon as I appear they are full of joy.'

347

The Swallow and the Serpent

A swallow who had nested inside a court of justice had flown off for a while. A serpent crept up and gobbled up her little ones. Finding the nest empty upon her return, she wailed, beside herself with grief. To console her another swallow told her that she wasn't the only one to have had the misfortune to lose her babies.

'Ah!' she replied, 'I am less distressed to have lost my young than that I should be a victim of a crime in a place where victims of violence should find help.'

This fable shows that ill luck or calamity is often more difficult to bear when it comes from those from whom one least expects it.

348

The Swallow and the Crow Obstinately Contending over Their Beauty

The swallow and the crow were disputing their beauty. To the swallow's argument, the crow replied:

'Your beauty flourishes only during the spring. But mine survives the winter.'

This fable shows that it is better to prolong one's life than to be beautiful.

349

The House-martin and the Birds

When the first mistletoe grew, the martin, sensing the danger which faced the birds, drew them all together and advised them urgently to cut off the mistletoe from the branches of the oaks where it grew; but, if that was not possible, to take refuge with men and beg them not to use mistletoe birdlime in order to trap them. The other birds laughed at the martin as being in her dotage. Hence she took herself off to live with men as a supplicant. They made her welcome for her intelligence and gave her a sanctuary at their homes. Thus it happened that the other birds were caught and eaten by men and only the martin, protected and sheltered by them, nests fearlessly even on their houses.

This fable shows that one escapes danger when one anticipates the future.

NOTE: The Greeks did not distinguish the swallow from the martin, so that the same word refers to both; in this case, evidently the house-martin seems to be referred to, as it was extremely common in ancient Greece. As for mistletoe, it rarely grows on oaks, but here it is assumed that it does, indicating that the fable was composed by someone who was not a countryman. There is another version of this fable, featuring an owl instead of a house-martin, preserved in the first century Rylands Papyrus, and the author Dio Chryso- stom also recounts that version. As for the use of mistletoe berries to make bird-lime to trap birds, we have encountered this before; see the note to Fable 137. See also Fables 157 and 242 for birdlime, and Fable 9 for house-martins.

350

The Boastful Swallow and the Crow

The swallow told the crow:

'I am a maiden, an Athenian, a princess, daughter of the King of Athens.'

And she went on to relate how Tereus had raped her and cut out her tongue. The crow retorted:

'What would you do if you had your tongue, when without it you chatter so much?'

Through lying, boastful people testify against themselves.

NOTE: See note to Fable 9. This fable is a joke based upon the mythological account of the rape of Philomela of Athens by the Thracian prince Tereus. Procne and Philomela were sisters, daughters of King Pandion of Athens. In return for assistance given in war, Procne was given to Prince Tereus in marriage. However, Tereus went back to Athens to fetch her sister Philomela, pretending that Procne had died. Then Tereus raped Philomela and, in order to prevent her telling anyone, he cut out her tongue. Procne learned of the rape because Philomela eventually wove a robe which depicted the scene and the event (note that it is presumed in the myth that the sisters were illiterate so that written communication was impossible).

The two sisters got their revenge by murdering Procne's son by Tereus, named Itys, and serving him up to Tereus to eat. Then Tereus changed into a hoopoe, Procne changed into a nightingale and Philomela became a swallow. Since this story was well known to all, the joke is that a boastful swallow is pretending to be Philomela.

351

The Tortoise and the Eagle

A tortoise begged an eagle to teach him to fly. The eagle pointed out that he was not made to fly – far from it! But the tortoise only pleaded with him even more. So the eagle took him in his talons, flew up into the air and then let him go. The tortoise fell on to the rocks and was smashed to pieces.

This fable shows that often, in wanting to compete with others in spite of wiser council, we can do ourselves harm.

352

The Tortoise and the Hare

The tortoise and the hare argued over which was the swifter. So, as a result, they agreed a fixed period of time and a place and parted company. Now the hare, trusting in his natural speed, didn't hurry to set out. He lay down at the side of the road and fell asleep. But the tortoise, well aware of his slowness, didn't stop running and, overtaking the sleeping hare, he arrived first and won the contest.

This fable shows that hard work often prevails over natural talents if they are neglected.

353

The Wild Geese and the Cranes

Some wild geese and cranes were foraging for food in the same wet grassland [*leimon*] when hunters suddenly appeared. The cranes flew off lightly but the geese, hindered by the heaviness of their bodies, were caught.

It is also like this with people; when a city is taken in war, the poor people easily save themselves by migrating from one land to another, thus preserving their liberty. But the rich are held back by the weight of their wealth and often become enslaved.

354

The Pots

An earthenware pot and a bronze pot were being carried downstream by a river. The earthenware pot said to the bronze pot:

'Swim away from me, not beside me. For, if you bump into me, I will burst into pieces; likewise if I touch you, even unintentionally.'

Life is uncertain for the poor person who has a rapacious ruler for a neighbour.

355

The Parrot and the House-ferret

A man who had bought a parrot let it fly freely in his house. The parrot, who was tame, jumped up and perched in the hearth, and from there began to cackle in a pleasant way. A house-ferret, seeing him there, asked him who he was and from whence he came. He replied:

'The Master went out to buy me.'

The house-ferret replied:

'And you dare, most shameless creature – newcomer! – to make such sounds, whereas I, who was born in this house, am forbidden by the Master to cry out, and if sometimes I do, he beats me and throws me out of the door!'

The parrot replied:

'Oh, go for a long walk! [i.e. get lost!] There is no comparison to be made between us. My voice doesn't irritate the master as yours does.'

This fable concerns all malevolent critics who are always ready to throw the blame on to others.

356

The Flea and the Boxer

One day, a flea landed with one jump on to the toe of a sick boxer, and took a bite of it. In a rage, the fighter prepared his nails ready to crush the flea. But it took off and, with its usual hop, escaped him and avoided death. So the boxer said with a sigh:

'Oh, Herakles! If that is the way you help me against a flea, what can I expect from you when I face my opponents?'

This fable teaches us that we too ought not to call upon the gods all the time for mere trifles, but for more urgent needs.

NOTE: This fable provides interesting evidence that the patron god of fighters and boxers may have been the deified strong-man, Herakles/ Hercules, although Herakles was also 'the Protector' in general to the common man.